Holiday Homecoming

Jean C. Gordon

D0032726

 HARLEQUIN® LOVE INSPIRED®

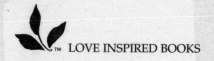

LOVE INSPIRED BOOKS

Recycling programs for this product may not exist in your area.

ISBN-13: 978-0-373-71925-9

Holiday Homecoming

www.Harlequin.com

Printed in U.S.A.

"You don't want to work on the pageant?" Connor asked her.

Natalie avoided his gaze. "It's just… Isn't it awkward for you? Wouldn't you rather be working with someone else?"

"We're both adults. Anything between us ended a long time ago. I agree with your mother that you're the best qualified person to step in for her."

"You didn't answer my question," she reminded him.

He wasn't sure he could. "I want the best person we can get for the choir director. You're good."

He lifted her chin with his forefinger. "What happened?" he asked suddenly. "Why are you really back?"

Connor was uncertain whether he thought it would help to talk about the elephant in the room.

Her eyes clouded. "This isn't easy to talk about."

"You don't have to. That was just counselor Connor kicking in. You know, all that listening and conflict resolution training I had at seminary."

"No, you're right. Talking will help us start over— as friends—so we can work together on the pageant."

Something in him rebelled at the way she emphasized *as friends*.

Jean C. Gordon's writing is a natural extension of her love of reading. From that day in first grade when she realized *t-h-e* was the word *the*, she's been reading everything she can put her hands on. Jean and her college-sweetheart husband share a 175-year-old farmhouse in Upstate New York with their daughter and her family. Their son lives nearby. Contact Jean at facebook.com/jeancgordon.author or PO Box 113, Selkirk, NY 12158.

Books by Jean C. Gordon

Love Inspired

The Donnelly Brothers

Winning the Teacher's Heart
Holiday Homecoming

Small-Town Sweethearts
Small-Town Dad
Small-Town Mom
Small-Town Midwife

"For surely I know the plans I have for you," says the Lord, "plans for your welfare and not for harm, to give you a future with hope."
—*Jeremiah* 29:11

To my family for being the anchor of my life
and putting up with my love of
celebrating holidays, any holiday.

Chapter One

If one more person tried to play matchmaker with him, Connor Donnelly didn't know what he'd do, but it might not be pastorlike.

Connor flipped his jacket collar up against the cold night air as he left the parsonage for the Christmas pageant practice he was supposed to be directing. Even his older brother, Jared—the man least likely to marry—had gotten into the matchmaker act since his wedding last summer. Connor shuddered at the memory of last weekend's blind double date.

Jared and his wife, Becca, had set him up with the younger sister of her college friend, who was in Ticonderoga on business. Becca had failed to tell the woman he was a minister. When it came up at dinner, she'd clammed up and made her exit as quickly as she could without being blatantly rude. It wasn't that Connor would mind being married. He'd just rather do the choosing and hadn't found a woman he cared strongly enough about, except...

Pushing that thought from his head, he drove the short distance from Hazardtown Community Church to the Sonrise Camp and Conference Center, where the practice was being held. He had more immediate things to occupy his time than his lame love life, like finding a replacement for Terry Delacroix, his church organist and the music director for the Paradox Lake churches' annual Christmas Eve pageant and ecumenical service. His church was sponsoring the service this year, making him the production director. Acing the production would help to solidify his standing with the small faction of his congregation who still weren't convinced Jerry Donnelly's son was the right pastor for Hazardtown Community.

As he opened the door to the newly built camp auditorium, he caught the end of a conversation between the twelve-year-old Bissette twins, who were standing in the hallway off the entry.

"She deserves a nice Christmas present, especially since Mom says she's getting her act together now. I think Pastor Connor would be perfect."

"Ye-e-es!" The second twin fist-bumped her sister.

Terrific, now the kids were getting in on it. He wasn't even going to speculate who the girls thought he'd make a perfect gift for.

Piano strains of "What Child Is This?" drifted from the auditorium, lifting Connor's spirits. It sounded like Drew Stacey, Sonrise's director, had gotten him a replacement. He owed his friend big-time. Connor strode into the auditorium anxious to see whom Drew had found.

"Pastor Connor," the twins called in unison, waving him to the front.

"Do you know our aunt Natalie?" Amelia asked.

"She's going to take Grandma's place for the pageant," Aimee finished for her sister.

The music stopped abruptly with a discordant sound.

Natalie turned slightly on the piano bench and looked out at Connor, an anxious expression on her face. When her gaze caught his, he tripped, grasping one of the seat backs to keep his balance.

Natalie Delacroix. The woman who'd broken his heart when she'd chosen her career over him and his marriage proposal.

That was five years ago. Ancient history, he mused as he walked the rest of the way down the aisle to the front of the auditorium.

"Hello, Natalie." The cool tone of his words surprised him, considering the battle of emotions that was going on inside him.

"Connor." Now that he was at close range, she wouldn't meet his gaze.

"You guys already know each other," one of the twins—Aimee, he thought—said.

"We went to high school together." And a lot more.

He glanced sideways at Natalie. She was staring at the sheet music in front of her as if the pages would disappear if she turned from them.

The other twin, Amelia, rolled her eyes. "We should have figured that."

The auditorium door opened. The girls squealed the name of one of their friends and went to join her, leaving him and Natalie alone.

"Are you visiting for the holidays?" he asked, again surprised at how calmly polite he sounded. The conflict-resolution training he'd taken in seminary was proving its worth.

Natalie gathered the sheet music and tucked it in a folder on the piano music stand. She was every bit as beautiful as she'd been that Christmas Eve five years ago, with her jet-black hair curling against her fair skin. Except something was missing.

"Dad and *Mémé* asked me to come and help Mom." She lifted her shoulders in a Gallic shrug he'd seen her French-Canadian grandmother use many times. "You know how much work the farm is for Dad and Paul, and *Mémé* isn't that well herself. Andrea's busy with her family and part-time job. Dad wanted someone with Mom during the day." Natalie tapped her fingers on the piano bench as she ticked off the reasons her other two sisters couldn't help. "Claire has her work at the research farm and she's taking grad courses, besides having used up most of her vacation time for the year. And it's not like Renee could take off from the mission in Haiti." She stopped tapping. "I had time. I'm between jobs. The station I was working at changed formats and didn't have a spot for me anymore."

Natalie spoke the words in a monotone. That was what was missing. Natalie's spark was gone. He looked at her more closely. Her features were sharper. She was thinner. Too thin. Faint slashes of blue under her eyes emphasized the tired look they held. His heart ached, as he wondered what was behind the changes. If she was simply one of his parishioners, he'd say something, see if she wanted to talk later. But with their history, he didn't know if he could help, or—even more—if she'd want him to.

He put on his professional face. "We've all been praying for your mother's speedy recovery. I'm sure she really appreciates your being here to help out." Like he would have appreciated Terry telling him Natalie was coming back to Paradox Lake for the holidays when he'd visited her in the hospital the day before yesterday.

"Thank you," Natalie said, holding herself straight-backed on the bench. "I'm glad I could come and help."

Connor shoved his fingers in the front pockets of his jeans. "Is she home from the medical center? I know she and your dad had a real scare with the postsurgical infection that caused her to be readmitted."

"Yes."

He could almost hear the silence following her terse reply. This was the same girl—woman—who used to chatter to him for hours, punctuating her words with animated hand motions?

"Connor," Drew Stacey called from the back of the auditorium, relieving him of having to try and make any more small talk. "I see you've met Terry's replacement."

The note of helpful pride in Drew's voice was unmistakable.

"From what Terry said, you and Natalie are old friends."

Connor nodded. *Were* friends, and a whole lot more.

In the silence, Natalie seemed to shrink into the piano bench.

"People are arriving. I'll get out of your way so you can get started," Drew said. "I'll be in the utility room working with the youth group on the stage settings. Give me a yell when you're done, and I'll lock up."

"Sure thing," Connor said. Drew's words made Connor aware of the din of people talking and moving in the auditorium behind them.

Drew turned to Natalie before he left. "The production is a little behind schedule. Practices usually get started the week before Thanksgiving, but your mom probably told you that. You still have a month. I'm sure the two of you can pull it off."

Natalie looked from Drew to him, her eyes full of question. Evidently, her mother hadn't told Natalie he was directing the pageant. Connor swallowed the lump that had formed in his throat. He'd worked hard to forgive and forget Natalie. Now here she was, her mere presence scratching through the top layers of self-protection he'd built. He had a feeling this December might be the longest month of his life.

Connor Donnelly. Her breath hitched. At one time, she and Connor had been so attuned to each other she could practically read his thoughts before he voiced them. Either he had become a lot better at controlling his expressions or she'd lost her touch. She had no idea what was going through his mind, except that she didn't think it was anything good. She waited for him to say something.

"I take it your mother didn't tell you that I'm directing the Christmas pageant," he said.

"No." So much for her hopes that being in Paradox Lake for the holidays would bring her some peace so she could start putting her broken life back together. Working with Connor would be anything but peaceful. Her mother had to know that. "I guess I assumed that since the pageant was here at the camp, Drew was in charge."

"Drew's just letting us use the camp auditorium. The local association of churches sponsors the pageant. The churches decided a few years ago that we'd get a better turnout for early Christmas Eve services if we combined forces with an ecumenical service for the young families, rather than having separate ones."

"That makes sense. How's it working?" she asked, hoping making small talk would calm the wildfires leaping from nerve ending to nerve ending.

"Good." His face became more animated. "We, the pastors, take turns directing."

Natalie felt a pinch of envy at his statement. She

didn't belong anywhere anymore, not even with her family. But she was glad he was part of something. Growing up with an alcoholic father who was frequently the center of local gossip, Connor and his two brothers had often felt they didn't fit in.

"It's my turn this year. We're going alphabetically by church." Connor stopped his explanation. "If you don't want to do this with me, say so."

Obviously, she'd failed in her efforts to pretend she could carry off a normal conversation with him.

"Your sister Andrea said she'd play if we couldn't find anyone else."

"No, it's fine. I told Mom I would."

Natalie searched his eyes to see if he'd thrown out Andie's name as a challenge. Quitting now and letting Andie swoop in to take over would be one more failure for Natalie in the eyes of her perfect oldest sister. But Connor wouldn't know that. He hadn't been around for her sister's regular phone calls lecturing her on how she and her lifestyle—or what Andie had pretty well perceived as Natalie's lifestyle—was hurting Mom and Dad. The calls hadn't started until after she'd broken up with Connor and followed her college mentor to Chicago to be a television news reporter.

"You know how I love Christmas music," she quickly added.

His mouth twisted in a half smile she couldn't decipher.

"Natalie! Is it really you?" Her high school friend Autumn Hazard—Hanlon now—rushed up to the front of the auditorium, relieving Natalie of having to continue to face Connor alone.

"It's me," Natalie said, glad to see Autumn, but embarrassed that she'd cut off contact with her the past couple of years. She only knew Autumn had married because her mother had told her.

"Aunt Jinx and Drew said you were filling in for your mother." Autumn grabbed Natalie's hands and pulled her to her feet. "Why didn't you let me know you were coming for the holidays?"

"It was a last-minute decision. Dad called, said he and Mom needed my help, and I came."

"I'm so glad to see you." Autumn hugged her.

Over Autumn's shoulder, Natalie watched Connor move away to join a group of people congregating in the aisle. He hadn't changed much since she'd last seen him. His dark blond hair was respectably shorter, the shoulders she'd leaned on maybe a little wider, and his facial features were more chiseled, making him resemble his oldest brother, Jared, and his father, rather than his mother, whom he'd looked like when he was younger. In other words, he looked good.

She couldn't say the same for herself, Natalie thought as Autumn stepped back to look at her.

"It's been way too long," Autumn said. "What, the summer after our sophomore year of college?"

"Probably," Natalie agreed. "I had an internship at WTVH in Syracuse the next summer, and after graduation, I moved to Chicago for work." The job she'd thought was her foothold into a career in television news that had turned out to be the path to the destruction of her career and personal life.

A loud whistle penetrated the din of voices in the room. "Time to get started," Connor said. "Sunday school kids, you can go out into the hall with Mrs. Donnelly, and she'll explain the parts she has available. Parents, after tonight, Becca will be having rehearsals on Saturday afternoons and one day after school, rather than at night. She has information she'll give the kids about transportation provided by the participating churches for anyone who needs it."

Becca led a swarm of kids and parents out of the auditorium. Natalie remembered her as Mrs. Norton, her high school history teacher. Strange to think she was Connor's sister-in-law now.

"Everyone else, up on the stage bleachers, bass in the back, then tenor, alto and soprano."

"I'll catch you later," Autumn said. "Our leader has spoken."

Natalie sat back down on the piano bench and watched the way everyone responded to Connor taking charge. He had a quiet command about him that she hadn't seen before.

"Many of you probably remember Natalie Delacroix." He pointed down at her and fifty or sixty sets of eyes followed his gesture.

Natalie forced herself to hold her head high and pasted her best onscreen smile on her face, wondering how much they knew about her and her fiasco in Chicago and what they might be thinking.

"Natalie has graciously agreed to take over as music director for her mother, who, for those of you who don't know, had emergency surgery the week before last. And be rest assured our music is in good hands."

She kept her gaze on the sheet music as Connor proceeded to tick off her qualifications.

"Eastman School of Music offered Natalie a scholarship before she decided to pursue a degree in broadcast journalism, and she minored in music at Syracuse."

Natalie bit her lip. She'd applied to Eastman to appease her mother, not because she'd wanted to pursue a music career. Music was something she did for fun. Unlike her career, music had always given her joy.

Someone started clapping and the whole group joined in. Natalie nodded her thanks. There was no way she could back out now.

"I know I asked you to line up according to your voice type, but for Natalie's benefit in choosing her accompaniment, please raise your hand when I say your voice type."

Connor ran through the four types and Natalie noted the numbers. It seemed like a fairly equal distribution, plus a few undecided.

She stood. Time to stop being a shrinking violet and start being the music director. Natalie pitched her voice to carry up to the back of the stage. "Those of you who aren't sure where your voice falls stop and see me after practice, and I'll have you test sing then or before our next practice if you can't stay tonight."

"Everybody got that?" Connor asked. "Natalie, your mother went over the selections the pageant committee agreed on?"

"Yes." She sat down and opened the music folder to the first song.

"Take it away, maestro," he said.

Natalie lifted her fingers and flexed them. "We'll warm up with 'Hark! The Herald Angels Sing.' I'll run though the first couple of stanzas. When I go back to the beginning again, you all join in."

She waited for Connor to leave now that the practice was beginning. Instead, he climbed the bleachers to the tenor section and stood in front of his brother Jared. A small tremor ran through her hands as she placed her fingers on the keyboard, remembering the rich timbre of his singing voice. Until she'd turned down his proposal Christmas Eve of her senior year, they'd driven to and from college together singing to the radio the whole way. The man could really do justice to a slow country ballad. She stopped a sigh. For whatever reason, she'd expected Connor to leave.

Natalie began to play, trying to lose herself in the music. But her mind kept running over ways to avoid being caught alone with Pastor Connor again.

She finally finished the program's closing song. "I think that's good for tonight." She paused. "Unless Connor has anything else."

"No, nothing except a reminder that the next practice is next Tuesday, same time."

A week. That gave her a week before she'd have to see Connor again. Except—the thought struck her—at church service. She shook off the feeling of uncertainty. What was with her? There wasn't anything between her and Connor anymore. She was a big girl. She could maintain a pastor-parishioner relationship with him. But he wasn't any ordinary pastor, and considering some of the stuff she'd gotten herself into the past couple of years, she was a far cry from his typical parishioner.

As she waited for choir members to check in with her about their range placement, a chuckle from Connor rose above the chatter, drawing her gaze to him. She followed his progress down the bleachers. The confident way he carried himself and the cordial expression on his face as he talked to those around him told her that Connor had finally found himself. Her heart warmed. She was happy for him. She could only pray that coming back might help put her on a calmer path, too.

Natalie tensed as Connor left the group and walked to the piano. She looked furtively for someone, anyone else, heading her way.

"Thanks again, Nat," he said, slipping into the familiar nickname only her family and friends in Paradox Lake used. "See you next week." He raised his hand in farewell as he walked past her and the piano.

"I'll be here." She released a pent-up breath and her anxiety about having to deal with him one-on-one flowed out with it. His short, politely distanced words were exactly what she wanted from him. So why did she feel a little more empty with each step he took away from her?

"So, what's with you and the piano player?" Jared accosted Connor as he headed toward the utility room to let Drew know that the choir was done.

"I can help with that one." His other brother, Josh, seemed to appear from the shadows. "Natalie was Connor's first love."

The mocking tone Josh put on the last two words ignited a spark of anger. "Where'd you come from?" Connor asked, forcing himself to ignore the taunt. This was Josh, after all. The man who'd never dated a woman long enough to have any feelings for her.

"I stopped by to help Drew and the kids with the settings. He gave me the key to give to you to lock up." Josh handed him a key ring. "Now, back to the beauteous Natalie Delacroix…"

Natalie was beautiful, and Josh was no longer mocking. Still, Connor had a childish urge to demand Josh "take that back," the kind of demand that had resulted in more than one teenage brother brawl.

"I think the lady dumped our baby bro their last year of college," Josh said.

"Something like that," Connor mumbled, glad that Josh didn't know the full story. Even though the two of them were close, Josh had a reckless streak that had stopped Connor from telling him beforehand that he was going to ask Nat to marry him, despite Connor having been certain at the time that she'd say "yes." That move had saved him from the embarrassment of having to share being shot down.

"You guys still on for helping me with the cottage Saturday morning?" Josh asked.

For once, Josh's habit of making things all about him didn't bother Connor.

"We'll be there," Jared said. "Brendon can't wait. I got him his own scaled-down tool belt."

Connor admired the way his oldest brother had bonded with his stepson and went out of his way to be a father to him in a way their father had never been to them.

"Connor?"

"Sure, as long as nothing more pressing comes up." Connor couldn't think of any reason right now that he wouldn't be able to help Josh work on the decrepit lakeside cottage he'd bought to fix up and sell. He was being contrary. Josh had a way of bringing the worst out in him.

His brother frowned.

"Like an emergency with one of my parishioners."

"Right. See you Saturday." Josh left.

"I'm going to do a walk around to make sure everything is turned off before I lock up," Connor said to Jared. "Catch you at Josh's Saturday."

"You can't get rid of me that easy," Jared said. "I need a lift home. I told Becca if she finished earlier than we did to go ahead home, and I'd get a ride from you."

"Pretty sure of yourself."

"Yeah."

Connor tossed his car keys at his brother. "Make yourself useful and go run the heater so the car's warm when I get out."

A couple of minutes later, Connor joined Jared. He put the car in Reverse to pull out of the parking space.

"Natalie Delacroix," Jared said out of nowhere. "I knew I recognized her."

Connor hit the brakes harder than necessary and skidded on the icy parking lot. Recognized her from where? She would have been eleven when Jared left Paradox Lake for the motocross circuit.

"When I was racing in the Midwest, she was a reporter on one of the local stations," Jared said.

Connor shrugged and put the car in Drive. "She had a mentor her senior year who was an anchor at one of the Chicago affiliate stations. He was a guest instructor at Syracuse. She'd talked about him helping her get a job when she graduated."

"No, this was a smaller, local station. But I'm sure it was her."

"Maybe. After we broke up, I didn't keep track of her. It was part of my 'get Natalie out of my system' program."

"That bad?" Jared asked.

"That bad." Connor considered telling him about his proposal, but thought again.

Jared nodded and went quiet for a couple of minutes. "Kirk Sheldon. Was that her mentor?"

"Sounds right." Connor knew it was right.

"You can take this for what it's worth. I only know what I read on the 'People' page of a suburban Chicago newspaper."

Connor glanced sideways at his brother. Jared looked like he was weighing whether to continue. "Since when do you read gossip pages?" he asked to fill the lull.

Jared glared at him. "Since my publicist suggested it. The page had a story about me that she'd wanted to make sure I read as a lesson in what I shouldn't be doing."

Connor snorted. "You're going to tell me there was a story about Natalie, too?"

"Do you want to hear this or not?"

He wanted to put his hands over his ears and shout *no*. "Go ahead," he said.

"It was before I caught her on TV that time. I didn't connect the two until now."

"I don't need background. Just the details." And the fewer, the better.

"The news anchor was estranged from his wife, an overseas correspondent, and apparently dating Natalie."

Natalie and her professor? Connor clenched his jaw. She'd gone on about Kirk this and Kirk that. He'd thought it was her usual chatter. Had she been two-timing him? The man had to be fifteen years older than them. He gripped the steering wheel until his hands hurt.

"I know the paper blew it all out of proportion. They always do." Jared stopped again. "To cut to the chase, the news anchor and his wife reunited and he publicly apologized for his indiscretions. Natalie was his latest. He stopped just short of naming names, but the writer insinuated that he was involved with Natalie. The story covered the reconciliation. 'Local anchor breaks love triangle and reconciles with wife,' or some such garbage. Natalie was collateral damage."

Poor Natalie. Despite his fresh hurt that she might have been interested in Kirk before they'd broken up, he wasn't going to judge. Only God could do that.

"I can't tell you what to do," Jared said. "But I'd take care."

Connor got the implied "concerning Natalie."

"Much as I hated the bad press I got when I was on the motocross circuit, parts of it were true. And the reputation I got from those stories hurt Becca. Your contract is up for renewal at the end of the year. Some of the members of the congregation are still warming up to your being Jerry Donnelly's kid. And I know how much serving here means to you. I don't want to see you get hurt."

"I'm a big boy. I can handle my own life." Connor yanked the steering wheel to turn into Jared's driveway and brought the car to an abrupt stop.

"See you Saturday," Jared said. He stepped out of the car and closed the door without waiting for Connor's response.

Good move on Jared's part. At the moment, he was inclined to blow off Saturday.

Connor drove home, parked his car in the parsonage garage and stepped out into the frigid night air. A vision of Natalie's drawn face and empty gaze shadowed him into the house. He knew he *should* give her a wide berth, not so much to protect his ministry at Hazardtown Community Church, but to protect his heart. And he would, starting tomorrow, once he'd gotten control over the concern for her that Jared's story had raised and his almost overpowering need to seek her out and shelter her in his arms.

Chapter Two

"Mom, sit down and let me do that." Natalie walked across the kitchen and lifted the spatula from her mother's hand. "What happened to your sleeping in and letting me take care of breakfast? Where's your walker?"

"By the table. I woke up and didn't see a light on in your room yet. Since I was awake, I thought I'd get things started."

Natalie looked at the clock over the kitchen sink that had been there as long as she could remember. Ten after five. "I would have been up in five minutes, anyway, if I hadn't heard you and gotten up."

"I've got bacon in the broiler and have already started cracking eggs to scramble. I'll just finish them."

Natalie took her mother by the shoulders, surprised at how delicate she felt under her hands, and helped her to the kitchen table. "Sit. I suppose you make breakfast for Claire, too, when she gets up for work. Seriously, you could set the coffeemaker and let them fend for themselves."

"I've been telling her that for years," her father said from the doorway. He walked over and kissed her mother on the cheek. "Not that I've had much success. How's it going for you?"

Natalie motioned to the table. "I have her sitting."

"I knew calling you was the right thing."

"Right back at you, Dad." She looked at her mother and father, who were still obviously in love after thirty-five years of marriage and six children. A warm cloak of safety wrapped around her. She could have used some of that inner security last night with Connor. If only it was something she could pocket and take with her when she left the house.

Natalie turned to the stove and finished breaking eggs into a bowl. She beat in some milk until they were smooth and sunny yellow.

"Oh, no, you're not letting Natalie cook." Her younger brother, Paul, one male half of the two sets of Delacroix twins—Paul and Renee, and Marc and Claire—walked in and sat at the table.

"And good morning to you, too." She poured the egg mixture into an iron frying pan.

"The last time I remember you cooking breakfast, you almost burned down the lodge at Sonrise."

"I did not," she protested.

"Sure you did. You volunteered to get up early and make pancakes for the church youth group at our annual campout. Mr. and Mrs. Hill were the leaders then." He prompted her memory. "A fawn or bird or something distracted you and you let the pancakes burn. The kitchen filled with smoke."

She remembered all too well. It wasn't a fawn or bird that distracted her. It was Connor splitting wood for the campfire planned for that evening. Contrary to Paul's embellishments, she didn't cause any fire, or fill the kitchen with smoke. However, the stack of blackened pancakes and Mrs. Hill stepping in to finish cooking breakfast were enough to win her razzing for the rest of the day. Connor had made it better, sitting with her at the campfire and stealing a kiss—their first—when the Hills weren't watching.

She suppressed the nostalgic longing for that more innocent time. "That was more than ten years ago. I've perfected my breakfast cooking since then." A faint whiff of well-done bacon drifted from the stove. She quickly opened the broiler and took the pan out.

"So I smell." Paul got in another good-natured dig. "You know I'm only teasing. We're all glad to have you home for the holidays."

"I'm glad to be here, too." Natalie placed the bacon on a plate, gave the eggs another stir and scooped them into a bowl.

"Dad and I are going to go cut a Christmas tree Saturday morning. Want to come along?"

Natalie smiled to herself. The annual trek to the local Christmas tree farm to find the perfect tree had always been one of her favorite holiday activities, one she'd missed the past few years. Last Christmas, she hadn't even bothered to put out the small ceramic table tree she had.

"Claire's coming," Paul said, adding Natalie's next oldest sister to the outing. "I don't know if Andie and Rob and the kids are."

"You don't have to talk me in to it," Natalie said. "You know I'll be there. I wouldn't miss Pharaoh Mountain Farm's mint hot chocolate for anything." *Even Andie being there.*

"Paul," their dad said, "if you have your social schedule all worked out, want to finish your breakfast and get to work?" He winked at Natalie.

Paul and his twin, Renee, were the most social of her and her five siblings, not that she and the others weren't social. Or at least, she had been social.

They guys polished off their food and left to start the morning milking.

"Want another cup of coffee, Mom?"

"You don't have to do that. It's not like I can't get up and walk over to the counter."

Natalie ignored the edge to her mother's voice. "I'm getting one for myself. I can refill yours. You should make the most of the special treatment. Who knows when you'll get it again?"

"You're right." Her mother handed over her coffee mug. "I have to admit that I'm not missing having to go to work every day, except for the people."

Natalie filled both mugs. "Any chance you could go part-time when you go back? You already have an almost full-time job with the farm books and business management."

Her mother pressed her lips together, making Natalie wonder if she'd overstepped the child-parent boundary by edging into her parents' financial situation.

"Milk prices have been uncertain, although the new yogurt plant in Amsterdam may help keep them more even. I figure I might as well hang on full-time until I can collect Social Security benefits."

That was more than ten years away. She wished she could help financially. That had been part of her dream of being a network news reporter, although she suspected her parents wouldn't accept help, even if she had the means to give it. At least she'd had enough money left from her cashed-out retirement plan account to come up with her share for the Hawaiian trip she and her siblings were giving their parents for Christmas. They had everything covered, down to someone to help Paul with the farm work. She couldn't remember the last time Mom and Dad had been away.

"Here you go." She handed her mother her coffee.

"Don't worry about us," her mother said. "You know your Dad wouldn't want to be doing anything else."

Natalie knew that, but she was more concerned about Mom.

"And Paul has some good ideas, like getting in on the yogurt deal, and he's taking over a lot of the management work I've always done."

"Good." She reached over and squeezed her mother's hand. "You need to concentrate on getting better."

Her mother squeezed back. "So, how did choir practice go last night?"

"About that." Natalie looked at her mother over the edge of her coffee mug. "Why didn't you tell me that Connor is the pageant director?"

"Because I was afraid you'd say no if I had. Right?"

"Maybe. Probably." She put her coffee down. "Drew Stacey said that Andie had offered to play if he couldn't find anyone else. Why didn't you let her? Connor. Me. You know what happened."

"Andie doesn't play or sing nearly as well as you do. I'm hoping you'll do the solo. Besides she has enough on her hands with the kids, helping Rob on the farm and her part-time job."

Her mother's last words stung, even though Natalie knew she didn't mean them in a hurtful way. Mom was stating fact. Until she found a new job, figured out her life, what did she have to do?

"And—yes, I'm interfering—you and Connor have some unfinished business. Working together might help you finish it."

Natalie's stomach churned as if her last swallow of coffee had been one too many. Yes, she and Connor did have unfinished business—at least she did with him. But she wasn't sure she had enough strength left in her to finish it. Nor was she certain anymore that God would give her that strength.

Connor stomped through the fresh dusting of snow that had arrived overnight to cover the parking lot of Pharaoh Mountain tree farm. With the clear blue sky and temperatures up near freezing, it was a perfect day to get a Christmas tree for the parsonage—for someone who wanted to get a Christmas tree. He, personally, hadn't had a tree ever. He knew it was childish, but Natalie refusing his proposal in front of the tree they'd just finished decorating together in her Syracuse apartment, complete with the Christmas star he'd given her for the top, had killed any interest he might have in putting one up for himself.

Last year, when Jared had been living with him, he and their then six-year-old half sister Hope had gotten one for the parsonage, and Becca and her kids had come over and helped decorate it. His only input had been to insist they put something other than a star on top. He couldn't see a flashing star atop a tree or anywhere else without seeing Natalie saying, "I'm sorry…" This year, he'd thought he was home free until the women heading up the church's hospitality and evangelism committees had decided it would be a good idea to have a community-wide open house at the parsonage the weekend before Christmas. All Connor had to do was supply the tree. They'd take care of the food and the rest of the decorating.

He gripped the saw he'd found hanging in the parsonage garage. He couldn't tell the women that he didn't want a Christmas tree in his house. So when Josh had canceled their workday to go into the office, Connor figured he might as well get it over with.

"Connor," someone called from behind, pulling him out of his morass. Claire Delacroix jogged up beside him, her cheeks turned rosy from the cold, just like Natalie's always had. "Picking up your Christmas tree?"

"That and some wreaths and boughs and stuff for the parsonage. The hospitality and evangelism committees are going to decorate for the open house."

"Want to join us? We're getting the tree for Mom and Dad's house."

"Sure," he said before considering who "we" might include. He hesitated. No, Natalie would be home, wouldn't she? In case her mother needed help.

"We're meeting at the chocolate hut," Claire said. "That's what we call the outbuilding where you pay for the trees."

His lack of knowledge of the tree farm must have shown on his face.

"You haven't been here before."

"No." At their house growing up, the tree had appeared Christmas Eve after they'd gone to bed. When he was older, he'd assumed Mom picked them up at a discount somewhere on her way home after she'd finished her Christmas Eve shift at the diner.

"They have the best hot chocolate with mint. Free with every tree. Don't tell Mom and Dad, but that's really why I got up early on a Saturday morning to come."

"Okay." He wasn't sure what all the excitement about hot chocolate was. His plan had been to get in and out as fast as possible.

Claire waved as they tromped toward a building the size of a large shed that looked like a miniature log cabin. Both of her parents, along with her brother Paul *and* Natalie, were standing in front.

"You should probably go ahead without me. I don't want to horn in on what sounds like a family tradition."

"Since when?" Claire laughed. "You used to be at the house so much, Mom called you her middle son."

"That was back in high school." He shoved his hands in the pockets of his ski jacket, fighting the old feeling of being an outsider that he'd thought he'd shed when he'd left Paradox Lake for college.

"Come on. It'll be a lot more fun with us than by yourself."

He walked over to the building with her. *Fun* wasn't exactly what he'd been expecting.

"Hey, look who I found in the parking lot," Claire said.

Almost in unison, Natalie's parents and brother gave him an enthusiastic greeting. Even Natalie smiled.

"I'm picking up a tree for the parsonage," he said. *Lame.* Why else would he be at a Christmas tree farm?

"For the open house." Terry nodded. "Where are you putting it? In the living room or the dining room? With the high ceilings at the parsonage, you'll want a tall tree."

Connor hadn't thought about the best place to put it. He just wanted to get the job out of way. "Last year, Jared and Becca put the tree in the living room."

"That's probably best," she said. "You'll have the buffet set up in the dining room."

The ladies will have the buffet set up. He was trying to stay as much out of the event as he could, putting his efforts where they belonged—on his Christmas church services and the pageant.

"The girls can help you." Terry's eyes twinkled with mischief, just as Natalie's used to. "They're both almost as good at picking out the right tree as I am. I'm going to wait here." She tapped her walker. "No hiking the hills for the perfect tree for me."

"I'll stay and keep you company," Natalie said. "Four people are enough to cut two trees."

Even though he'd been looking for an out minutes ago, hearing Natalie say the same thing sharpened already painful memories.

"And miss the fun? No way. Go ahead," Terry urged. "I'm fine here with my hot chocolate."

Natalie opened her mouth and closed it.

"The taller trees are in the back," Natalie's father, John, said. "That's where we're headed."

Connor fell in step with Natalie's brother at the opposite side of their little group. "How's it going, Paul?"

"Not bad." Paul glanced at his father, who was talking with the girls. "I talked Dad into getting in on the deal supplying milk for the new yogurt plant. Andie's husband, Rob, is in, too."

"Great." Connor knew how much Paul was working on making his partnership with his dad more of a partnership.

"And with Natalie here and Marc and his family coming Christmas Eve, we'll all be home except Renee."

Connor caught a note of sadness when Paul said his

twin's name. "Are you going to be able to use Skype to talk with her?"

"Yep, we're planning to Christmas morning."

"Here we are. Take your pick," John said when they'd reached the far end of the farm.

"Natalie, why don't you help Connor? It'll give you two time to catch up," Claire said. "I'll make sure these two guys don't go overboard on tall." She motioned to her dad and brother.

Connor glanced at Natalie. She quickly turned the grimace her sister's words had caused into a facsimile of a smile. He crushed an ice ball from one of the trees that had fallen in his path. Her stifled displeasure affected him far more than it should. What did he care if she didn't want to come with him? She had no hold on him. He was over her, had been for years.

"Sorry about that," Natalie said as soon as her family was out of hearing range. From his expression, Connor might be even less happy about her family throwing them together than she was apprehensive about it. Not that she blamed him.

"I'm used to it," he said. "People are always trying to match me up with single women."

And that's all she was, one more potential match pushed at him. She shivered despite having bundled up for the weather. Had any of those matches worked? She hadn't heard he was seeing anyone. Unjustified jealousy shot through her. She shook it off. Any chance she'd had of being anything to Connor, even friends, had died five years ago when she'd chosen her career over his proposal. They'd been so young. She felt decades older and knew now that it hadn't had to be an either/or.

"What kind of tree are you looking for, long or short needle?" she asked.

"You're the expert."

The lopsided grin that had replaced his frown went straight to her heart. How many times had she succumbed to that grin and agreed to watch the movie he wanted to see or eat out at his favorite restaurant or help him clean his apartment?

"Well, the short-needled trees tend to hold their needles longer. But if you like the looks of a longer needle…"

He touched the sleeve of her navy peacoat. "It's okay. I was teasing. I know you're as uncomfortable as I am."

Uncomfortable. He sounded so clinical. And she was being oversensitive. Connor was handing her the olive branch she should be giving him, the branch she didn't even know how to offer him. Memories flooded her head. Them in the parking lot of the big-box store near her apartment in Syracuse looking at the meager selection of trees left for sale. They'd chosen a long-needled white pine that had started shedding its needles before they'd even set it up. Her making him laugh with stories of tree mishaps she remembered from her childhood as they decorated the tree.

She nodded, afraid that if she spoke, she'd give away emotions she didn't want Connor to see, that he probably wouldn't want to see.

"Since the tree will have to make it through at least a month, I'd better go with something with short needles," he said.

"The short-needled balsam firs are to the right." She pointed in the direction her family had gone, thankful that Connor was back to business. They walked over to the row of trees.

Connor stopped in front of the first one. "This one looks good." He started to squat to cut it.

"No, wait." She should let him go ahead and be done with it. But she couldn't without walking around it to inspect the tree from all angles. Too many tree-cutting trips with her mother stopped her from letting him cut the tree.

"What?" A note of impatience sounded in his voice.

She walked around the tree, telling herself this was the parsonage tree. She was being fussy because it needed to be right for the church, not because she wanted it nice for Connor.

"No good," she said as she rounded back beside him. "It lists to the side. You'll have trouble keeping it up, and I noticed some holes in the branches in the back. The trees at the end of the row are probably less picked over."

He straightened. "Lead on."

She stepped in front of him and walked slowly down the row, eyeing each tree, the scent of pine bolstering her spirits. Picking out a perfect Christmas tree was something she'd always liked, enjoyed sharing with her mother. Natalie stopped at the far end of the row.

"This one?" Connor asked.

"No." Her gaze traveled to the next row. "There." A twinge of excitement bubbled as she pointed. Without thinking, she grabbed his arm to pull him over.

He stilled for a moment, his blue eyes clouding.

She dropped her hand to her side.

"Which one?" he asked with what sounded to her like forced enthusiasm.

"Next row, second one in." Natalie rushed over and circled the tree. "It's perfect."

Connor laughed, sending a ripple of remembrance through her.

"I'll have to move all of the furniture out of the living room and cut a hole in the ceiling to fit it in," he teased.

"No, you won't. All you'll need to do is trim some of the wide branches on the bottom and take a foot or so off the trunk, like you had to with the tree at my apartment."

Connor's stance stiffened. Why did she have to go and say that when they'd finally reached a friendly comfort?

Without a word, Connor attacked the tree trunk with the saw he'd brought. Natalie watched his shoulders work as he pulled back and forth, and she lifted a silent voice rusty with disuse. *Dear Jesus, I know I have to talk with Connor, clear the air between us if we're going to work together on the pageant to glorify Your birth. But I have no idea how to do it.*

Chapter Three

When Connor got back to the parsonage, he stuck the tree in a bucket of water in the far corner of the garage. No need to have it in the house until the church women came to decorate.

His cell phone pinged. It was a text from Josh: Got done early. You still up for some demolition?

Definitely, he texted back. Ripping out wallboard with his bare hands sounded like just what he needed to work the memories Natalie had dredged up this morning out of his system. He grabbed his toolbox and headed over to Josh's place.

A while later, his little sister, Hope, skipped into the room of the cottage he and Josh were gutting. "Hey, Connor, I'm going to hang out with you tonight."

"Hope, hon." He stopped her halfway across the debris-covered floor. "It would be better if you stayed back in the other room. I don't want you to get hurt."

Jared appeared in the doorway. "Hope," he said in a much sterner voice than Connor had used. "I told you to wait for Brendon and me."

She blew her bangs off her face. "But I didn't want

Connor to make other plans before I told him I was having a sleepover at his house tonight. If he has his cell phone, someone could have called him while I was waiting."

Connor couldn't argue with her seven-year-old logic.

"Hope," Jared repeated.

Connor brushed the plaster dust off his jeans. It bothered him that Jared often ended up playing the bad guy to their sister because she lived with him and Becca, while he and Josh got to be the fun brothers. Although Jared was Hope's legal guardian in their missing father's absence, they'd agreed to share responsibility of the motherless girl when her guardian grandmother had died last year.

Hope retraced her steps back to the doorway where Jared stood. "So is it okay, Connor?" she asked. "You're not doing something else?"

"Not a thing. What do you say we pick up subs on our way home for supper?"

"Can I pick out my own kind? At home, Ari and I have to take turns choosing since we always have to split one."

"Life is tough at the Donnelly household," Jared commented.

Not anywhere near as tough as it had been at theirs growing up.

"As long as it's not the veggie one, since I'm the one who'll have to finish the other half if you can't."

Hope wrinkled her nose. "Never. And I brought some games and stuff to do."

"Great."

Her expression turned serious. "Josh, don't feel left out. I can come to your house next Saturday."

Connor had to work at not bursting out laughing as he watched Josh struggle to keep a grin off his face.

"It's a date," Josh said. "We can go to the Strand and catch a movie."

"Bro," Jared said, "you've been spending a lot of time at the movies. Or is that a lot of time with the theater owner?"

Josh shrugged him off. "What can I say? She lets me watch the movies from the projection room."

"Cool! Can we do that next week?" Hope asked.

"I'll check with Tessa," Josh said, "but I don't see why not."

"Hey, guys. I thought we were here to work, not discuss Josh's love life," Connor said in an effort to deflect Josh before he decided to move on to him and Natalie. Connor had ignored, not missed, the gleam in Josh's eye when he'd filled in Jared on his and Natalie's former relationship the other night.

"Yeah," Josh said. "I want to get this room walled in today. It's Saturday, and some of us who aren't old and married have plans for the night."

Connor guessed Josh's plans were more adult than his. His insides hollowed. Maybe he should start taking up some of his parishioners on their matchmaking, if for no other reason than to get some woman other than Natalie in his thoughts.

"Brendon, set Hope up with her art stuff in the other room," Jared said, "and we'll see what Uncle Josh has for you to do."

His brothers would probably laugh if they knew how much he liked Becca's son and her daughter, Ariana, calling him Uncle Connor instead of Pastor Connor. It gave him a feeling of family that he hadn't had growing up in their too-often chaotic household.

"Josh, don't you have something I can do, too?" Hope asked.

"No, you're too little," Brendon said in the true fashion of an older brother, even though he actually was Hope's nephew by marriage.

"It just so happens I do," Josh said. "The box with my nails and screws and bolts is a mess. You could sort through them and put the ones that are alike together in the different compartments."

Jared gave a thumbs-up behind Hope.

"Brendon, it's in the back hall where you came in," Josh said. "You can carry it for Hope."

"Thanks, guys," Jared said after the kids had headed to the hall. "Ari went home with a friend after play practice this morning, and Brendon's staying over at his friend Ian's tonight. Hope was feeling left out."

Jared didn't have to add what the three brothers were all thinking. *I know how that feels.* Connor learned young that because of their father, they couldn't have friends over. His behavior was too unpredictable. And not being able to ever reciprocate made for fewer invitations to other kids' houses.

"And I'll have you know, Josh," Jared said, "since us old marrieds are kidless tonight, I have some Saturday night plans, too."

Josh threw up his hands in mock surrender. "I concede, maybe you aren't all of the way over the hill. Yet."

Connor grabbed the broom from the gutted wall beside him. He swept a section of the floor large enough to roll out and cut the batt insulation. If not for his little sister, he'd be left out—again.

Brendon popped back in the room. "So, what can I do?"

"You can help Uncle Connor measure and cut the insulation." As usual, Jared took charge. "Josh and I'll staple it up."

Relegated to the easy job as he always had been, being the youngest. Connor stalked across the room, heaved a roll of insulation on his shoulder and crossed back to the spot he'd swept. He let the roll drop to the floor.

"Think fast." Josh shot a tape measure at him. By reflex, Connor reached his hand above his head and caught it. He was acting as childish as Hope, only she had reason to. She *was* a child. He pulled out the tape and let it snap back in. He was a grown man, secure in his profession, secure with who he was. Or he had been until Natalie had returned.

She'd caught him by surprise, and that surprise had somehow stripped him of all the confidence he'd built in himself at seminary through prayer and hard work. It had also washed away the foundation of the wall he'd put up to keep her out of his thoughts. Natalie was seeping in them all too often. *Like now.*

"I don't get to use tools or anything?" Brendon complained.

"Hey, bud, you don't need hammers and staple guns to do a man's work. Our part of the job is the thinking man's part. Jared and Josh's is just grunt work."

Brendon eyed him.

"If we don't measure and cut the insulation right, it won't work right and the room will be drafty." Connor sliced the roll open with a utility knife.

Brendon probably bought that as much as he bought his plan to keep Natalie out of his head by avoiding her as much as possible outside of the pageant. Look at how well that had worked this morning.

"Nat, you have to do me a favor." Andie had started the phone call without even saying *hello*. "You have to fill in for me this afternoon decorating the parsonage for the open house. Robbie is sick."

Natalie's nephew had seemed okay an hour ago at church service. Was her sister purposely trying to make her uncomfortable by pushing her to go help Connor decorate his house?

"He's had the sniffles, but now he's spiked a temperature. If it goes higher, I'm going to have to take him to urgent care."

Natalie twisted her hair around her finger, her throat tightening with concern for the four-year-old. She was doing what Andie often accused her of—making it all about herself. "Sure. What time?"

"Two thirty."

That only gave her an hour to prepare herself. "Will Connor be there?"

"I don't know. Probably. You're not still carrying a torch for him after all these years, are you? You lost your chance when you let him get away in college."

No, no torch. Only regrets for her callousness. But leave it to big sis to go right for the jugular without even meaning to. "I need to check a couple things with him about the pageant music."

"Oh. Thanks for doing this. The twins were going to come with me, so I'll have Rob drop them off at the parsonage. That way you don't have to come out of your way to pick them up. You'll just have to drive them home. Dad was right when he said having you here for the holidays would be a help for us all."

Natalie was sure Andie's take on Dad's words wasn't exactly what he'd meant. "Hope Robbie feels better," she said, then ended the call.

"Bad news?" her mother asked.

Natalie almost dropped her phone. "Mom! I thought you were resting."

"I tried. It doesn't feel right, lying in bed during the day."

"You need to be careful not to put too much stress on your knee. Sit down at least." She helped her mother from her walker onto the couch.

"You're changing the subject. Something's wrong. You didn't get called back to work, did you? You said it was no problem to take family leave."

No, no problem at all. Natalie didn't know how to start. "I don't have a job," she blurted.

Her mother patted the spot beside her. "They called you on a Sunday afternoon to tell you that?" Outrage colored her words. "You're on family leave. I thought that gave you job protection."

Natalie dropped onto the couch. "I lost my job several months ago."

Her mother hugged her shoulder. "More downsizing?"

Good old Mom, always thinking the best of her, of all of them. It wouldn't occur to her that Natalie would be fired or quit a job without having another one lined up.

"Sort of," she said. "This time, the station was sold and the new owners wanted a different format with different people." Natalie scraped her nail against the knobby fabric of the armrest. Might as well get it all out. "I didn't lose the one before that because of downsizing. I was fired for not doing what was asked of me."

Her mother knit her brows. "That doesn't sound at all like you," she said, concern clouding her face.

"You don't know what was expected."

"Tell me."

Natalie's chest tightened until she could barely draw a breath. "I can't. I made a poor choice in my personal life, and I paid for it." Connor's face flashed in front of her. *A couple of bad choices.*

"We've all made bad choices, and God forgives us for every one of them."

Natalie couldn't imagine her dear mother making the choices she'd made.

"How bad is it?" Mom asked.

She might as well tell all, at least as much as she could bear to share with her mother. "I had to give up my apartment a couple of months ago, and I used the last of my savings for my plane ticket here and some Christmas gifts."

"You didn't have to bring gifts. Having you here is enough for all of us."

"Thanks, Mom, but I wanted to, especially for the kids." *And for you and Dad.*

"If I'm not prying, where have you been living?"

"A friend from the women's Bible study at church invited me to move in with her."

Mom nodded. "I'm glad you've been able to hang on to your faith."

"I've been trying, Mom. It hasn't been easy."

"It often isn't. When I'm having trouble hanging on, I quote *Lamentations 3:24-25* to myself. 'The Lord is my portion; therefore I will wait for Him. The Lord is good to those whose hope is in Him, to the one who seeks Him.' Waiting has always worked for me."

She hugged her mother, feeling for the moment that she was safe from the ruthless world she'd left to come home, that she was somewhere she belonged.

Her mother patted her back as she drew away. "So why *were* you frowning at your phone when I came in?"

Natalie released a laugh that bordered on maniacal. "Andie called and asked me if I could fill in for her helping the women from church decorate the parsonage this afternoon. She thinks Robbie is coming down with something."

"I hope not," her mother said. "I'll call her later to check on him. And you'll have a good time helping decorate. It's a younger group of women than what you'd remember. Autumn and Becca and some other girls you may know from school will be there."

"It's not that." Natalie's voice dropped to a whisper. "It's Connor's house."

Her usually perceptive mother cocked her head in question.

Natalie's throat clogged. "I treated him badly. Every time I see him, I feel like I should apologize, do something to make it up to him." She waved her hands as if grasping for an answer. "But I don't know how, what."

"You're not the only young woman who's turned down a marriage proposal, and you're not the only one who's had second thoughts afterward."

Natalie chose to skip over her mother's last words. "But I wasn't nice about it. In my eyes, he'd become too small-town, and I had cities to conquer. I'm sure I made him feel that being a television reporter was more important than anything he could offer, that he and his proposal would get in the way of my career."

A raw laugh caught in her throat. *Some career.* She'd

been so naive. And in the far recesses of her mind, she'd harbored the thought that he'd always be there for her to fall back on. She hadn't seen him again after that Christmas Eve until the other night at the pageant practice.

"I'm going to let you in on a secret. I turned down your father's first proposal. He asked me on my birthday, just before our high school graduation. He had it all mapped out. We'd move to Cobleskill and I'd work while he did his two years of agriculture school. Then, we'd come back and he'd work the farm with your grandfather."

"But…" Natalie started. Her parents had gotten married the summer after Dad had finished his two-year ag degree.

"Let me finish. I had bigger things to do, like make the US ski team. And I would have if I hadn't torn up my knee," her mother said matter-of-factly. "But God had other plans. Despite my refusing his proposal, your dad was with me as much as he could be after that surgery, as he has been with this one." She motioned to her knee brace.

"Connor's and my situation is different."

"I don't know. I was hurting. You're hurting. Talk with Connor. See where it goes."

Mom meant well, but Natalie knew where it would go. Nowhere.

I'm not the girl he wanted anymore. And Connor has become everything I'd expected he'd become and rashly thought I didn't want.

Connor sawed the trunk of the evergreen above the pail-shaped block of ice and attacked the lower branches to expose enough trunk for the tree to sit securely in the tree stand. He probably shouldn't have left the tree in the pail of water overnight. But who knew the church women could organize their work day so quickly? One of them must have seen Natalie and him cutting the tree yesterday. An email was waiting for him when he and Hope had gotten home from Josh's asking if there was any problem with them decorating this afternoon.

He partially sawed the last branch. Sometimes he thought his parishioners took advantage of his time, thought he was always available because he didn't have a family. He ripped the branch from the tree. But he was supposed to be available. That came with the job. He glanced at Hope, sitting on the steps from the house into the garage watching. He did have a family. After she'd heard him announce the parsonage decorating at church, she'd asked him if she could stay today, too.

"What do you think?" He held the tree upright for Hope.

"It's big. We don't have a tree yet. Becca said we'll get one next weekend when everyone is home and can go. Since I'm going to help decorate your tree, do you want to come over and help us decorate ours?"

Connor didn't want to participate in decorating this tree, let alone another one. "I'll see. I never know when I might be called to help someone."

"I know," Hope said with a deep sigh. "Cami Hill's grandmother—remember, she was my old day-care teacher before Jared and Becca got married—said you could really use a helpmate."

Add another church member to the "get Pastor married" brigade.

"What's a helpmate?" Hope asked.

"Someone who helps you do stuff," he answered, knowing Karen Hill's definition was really a wife.

"I can be your helpmate today," Hope said.

His heart warmed. "Yes, you can, starting with helping me move these tree branches out of the garage and into the woods behind the house."

Hope hopped off the steps while he lifted the garage door.

"Hi, Pastor Connor." The Bissette twins walked up his driveway as their dad's truck pulled away.

"We're here to help decorate your house. Dad had to drop us off early. One of the cows hurt her leg, and he has to get back to meet the vet."

"Me, too," Hope said. "I'm being Connor's helpmate. Do you want to, too?"

Aimee and Amelia giggled, reminding him of their conversation he'd overheard at the pageant practice saying he'd make a good Christmas present for their aunt Natalie. He rubbed his neck under the collar of his ski jacket, glad for the blast of cold air that blew into the garage. He must have exerted more energy than he'd thought cutting the tree branches.

"We need to haul these branches out back," he said, belatedly realizing the twins were alone. "Your mother didn't come?"

"No," Aimee said. He identified her by her name knitted into her ski cap. "Robbie is running a temperature."

"So Mom's making Aunt Natalie come," Amelia finished for her sister. "We're supposed to meet her here."

"Making Natalie come" was probably right. After yesterday's tree cutting, he couldn't see Nat volunteering to come and decorate his house. He also had trouble with the idea of Natalie doing something she didn't want to because Andie had told her to. The Natalie he used to know, at least. Thinking back, though, had he really known her then, either?

"Grab some branches," he said. "I want to get the garage cleared out and the tree in the house before everyone else gets here."

Several cars were parked in the driveway and women were milling around the garage when Connor and the girls walked back around to the front of the house. A quick check didn't find Natalie among them. He flexed the tightness out of his shoulders. Maybe he'd have time to escape to his office before she arrived.

"Hi. We were hauling the branches I trimmed from the tree out back. You could have gone in. The door's open." He bounded up the stairs and held the door open for his parishioners and the girls. "I'll get the tree and be right in."

He stared at the tree, his stomach flip-flopping in an all-too-familiar way, as it had when he'd gotten off the school bus as a kid and seen his father's truck in the driveway, not knowing what condition he'd be in. Connor grabbed the tree and dragged it through the kitchen and dining room to the living room.

"I see you brought down the tree stand," Karen Hill said. "Did you get the decorations, too?"

He didn't know there were any decorations. He'd thought Jared and Becca had used their own decorations last year.

"There should be a big box or two of decorations church members and former pastors and their families have donated over the years."

"I'll go check," he said, glad for the escape.

"I'll help you," Hope volunteered. When they'd gotten the tree stand down yesterday evening, she'd been fascinated by the attic, from the trapdoor in the upstairs hall to the pull-down ladder stairs.

"Okay." He and Hope could get the decorations, and then he could make his excuses and go work in his office. Karen and the twins would be more than happy to keep an eye on Hope.

When they got upstairs, he opened the outer trapdoor, unfolded the ladder stairs and climbed up two so he could reach the latch on the inner insulated trapdoor. The second door had been installed as an additional heat barrier when the attic was insulated several years ago. He pulled it open, making sure he snapped the lock brace so it wouldn't close on them while they were in the attic. With all the insulation, any calls for help might be so muffled no one downstairs would hear them.

"You go first," he said. "Hang on to the rails."

Connor followed Hope and quickly found the box of decorations, along with another box marked "manger."

"Here's another one," Hope said, holding up a small box marked "Christmas." "I'm getting good with my reading, aren't I?"

"Yes, you are. I'm going to take the three boxes down. Then you can come down."

"But I'm going to carry my box down the real stairs," Hope said.

He stacked the boxes in order of size and maneuvered his way down the ladder, placing them on the floor so his hands were free if Hope needed help. They carried the boxes down to the living room.

He placed the decoration and manger boxes next to the tree, which the women had already put in the stand while he was upstairs. "Karen, would you mind keeping an eye on Hope? I have some work to do in my office."

"Making a run for it?" Karen said.

He was that obvious?

"I'm teasing," she added.

His expression must have given away his guilt. After all, it was his house, his tree. A piece of him felt he should be a part of the decorating, despite the toll on his equilibrium.

"It's no trouble," she said.

"We'll help," the twins said.

"We've taken the babysitting class at the library," Amelia added.

"Thanks. If you need me for anything, give a shout."

As he made the turn at the stair landing, he heard one of the twins say, "Aunt Natalie, finally," sounding a lot like Natalie's oldest sister. The knot in his stomach that had been tying and untying all afternoon loosened, replaced by his inner voice repeating "coward" with each step he climbed away from her.

"Look what I found in the attic," Hope said, lifting a silver-and-blue star from a box.

Natalie's heart stopped. It was the star Connor had bought for her Christmas tree. She hadn't had the heart to use it or throw it away. It must have been in one of the boxes of stuff she'd brought home from college before she'd moved to Chicago. A few years later, she'd told Mom to go ahead and donate or give away anything in the boxes. It hadn't occurred to her Mom might add it to the parsonage Christmas decorations.

"Plug it in, Aimee," Hope said. The star twinkled with diffused light. "It's beautiful. Connor is going to love it."

"No," she blurted before she could stop herself. "I

mean that's an old decoration. Wouldn't you like to go with Connor and help him pick out a brand-new one?" Several of the women looked at her strangely. But she couldn't let Connor come down and see that star on his tree.

"No," Hope retorted as sharply as Natalie. "It's beautiful, like the one my grandmother and me had, and Connor is going to love it."

"Sweetie..." Natalie touched Hope's shoulder.

She pulled away. "Leave me alone." The little girl jumped up and ran upstairs, hugging the star to her chest.

Natalie rose, helpless to corral her emotions into any action that would make sense to the women around her.

"Let her go," Karen said. "Connor has a room that's hers upstairs. She's probably overtired. Hope was telling my daughter-in-law in Sunday school class that she and Connor had a big night last night and he let her stay up way later than Jared and Becca do."

"All right." Karen knew more about kids than she did. Natalie set to work untangling the intertwined strings of lights, a nice mindless job.

A while later, Amelia tracked down Natalie in the kitchen as she was getting a bottle of water from a cooler of drinks one of the women had brought.

"I went upstairs to see if Hope wanted to come back down and help decorate the tree and I couldn't find her. I think she went up to the attic. Someone left the ladder down."

"Did you look for her there?"

"No, you have to climb a ladder. Remember, I'm afraid of ladders."

Amelia had fallen off the ladder to the hay mow when

she was a toddler and broken her arm. But it surprised Natalie that she still had a fear of ladders.

"Does Co— Pastor Connor know?"

"No, I didn't want to tell him. We said we'd watch her."

"Where's Aimee? Can she check the attic?" She hated that she couldn't stop herself from coming up with ways to avoid going upstairs where Connor was.

"She went with Autumn to get some more tree boughs."

"Okay, I'll look in the attic." If Hope wasn't there, she was probably in Connor's office with him. It was unlikely she could have come downstairs and gone outside without anyone noticing.

Natalie put the unopened water back and walked unnoticed through the living room and upstairs, giving her second thoughts about Hope not being able to slip outside. Her heart pounded as she passed the closed door that must be to Connor's office. Afraid that Hope wouldn't answer if she called up to her, Natalie climbed the ladder. "Hope," she said as she stepped from the ladder into the room.

"Natalie?" Connor's voice came from behind a stack of boxes on the other side of the room.

Her heart slammed against her chest. "Amelia told me she thought Hope was up here."

Connor crisscrossed the maze of boxes and furniture to her. "She told me the same thing, and that she's afraid of ladders."

"The ladder part may be true."

"Let's get out of here," he said in as angry a tone as she'd ever heard from him.

Before they could move, the inner trapdoor slammed closed, followed by a muffled giggle.

Chapter Four

Connor sensed Natalie hovering behind him as he pressed his palm against the trapdoor. It didn't budge.

"You can open it, right?" she asked.

He didn't know, but hearing the strain in her voice, he wasn't going to say that. He straightened and pulled his Swiss Army knife from the front pocket of his jeans. "Your niece must have flipped the latch. I'm going to see if I can unscrew the hinges."

Natalie stood next to him and glared at the trapdoor. "I don't know what's gotten in to Aimee and Amelia."

Connor unfolded the screwdriver tool from the knife and kneeled on the floor. "The twins think I'd make a good Christmas gift for you." He placed the screwdriver in the slot of the closest hinge screw.

"What?" she said so loudly that if the attic wasn't so well insulated, everyone downstairs would have heard her, and they wouldn't have to worry about getting out of the attic.

"I overheard them before the pageant practice the other night," he said.

As she crossed her legs on the floor, her knee brushed

his leg. His knife slipped out of the screw. Not that the slight contact had rattled him. No, it was a Phillips screw and the knife had a slot screwdriver tool.

"I'll talk to the twins and to Andie."

"No need to make a big deal about it." Her lack of any reference to what the twins had said hit him in the pit of his stomach. He didn't know why he'd even said anything. What did he expect her to say—*best Christmas gift ever*?

"I could talk with Andie about taking over directing the choir, too."

Connor torqued the screwdriver to the left. It slipped out of the groove again and he grazed his knuckle against the metal hinge. He started to lift his hand to his mouth and stopped. "You don't want to work on the pageant?" *Or you don't want to work with me?*

She avoided his gaze, resting her elbows on her knees, chin on her crossed hands, eyes focused on the trapdoor. "It's just… I mean…isn't it awkward for you? Wouldn't you rather be working with someone else?"

"We're both adults. Anything between us ended a long time ago. I agree with your mother that you're the best qualified person to step in for her."

"You didn't answer my question."

No, he hadn't.

She lifted her head as if to challenge him to.

He wasn't sure he could. "The pageant and church service are my job. I want the best person we can get for the choir director. You're good. You could have majored in music, probably been a professional pianist if you'd wanted to. What more could I, Hazardtown Community Church and the Paradox Lake Association of Churches ask for?" He gave the screw another hard twist and the screwdriver snapped.

"Maybe I should have majored in music and saved everyone a lot of grief." She lowered her gaze to the trapdoor, her thick black lashes brushing her cheeks.

He scooped up the broken screwdriver tool before she could see it. The quaver in her voice told him it wasn't the time to tell her they were trapped up here. He shoved the broken tool in his pocket and lifted her chin with his forefinger. "Was it that bad? What happened?" Connor was uncertain whether he thought it would help to address the elephant in the room, or if he was hoping to hear her disprove what Jared had told him.

Her eyes clouded. "This isn't easy to talk about."

"You don't have to. That was just Counselor Connor kicking in. You know, all that listening and conflict-resolution training I had at seminary."

"No, you're right. Talking will help us find grounds for starting over—as friends—so we can work together on the pageant."

Something in him rebelled at the way she emphasized "as friends," as if she could wash away everything that had been between them by telling her story, and they could pick up being the friends they'd been back in high school. It might normally be his job, but he didn't want to be her confessor. She wasn't one of his parishioners. She was his first and, so far, only love. The woman who'd trashed his heart. He clenched his jaw, waiting for her to continue.

"First," she said, chipping at what was left of the pink polish on her thumbnail, "I need to apologize for the thoughtless way I turned down your proposal."

Need to, not *want* to. It was only semantics, but in

Connor's mind, Natalie's word choice made the situation all about her.

"You caught me by surprise. I hadn't realized you were that serious about us. We were so comfortable with each other."

Comfortable. Not exactly the top way he'd choose to be described. Connor sat back and stretched his legs out across the trapdoor.

Concern flickered across Natalie's face as she looked from the door he'd been trying to open to him. "It was because of something Kirk—Kirk Sheldon, my professor—said." She seemed to choke on his name.

"I remember him," Connor said without showing any of the rancor he felt, despite the twist of anger in his gut.

"He'd been talking to the class about the anchor job he had waiting for him in Chicago and how the station expected to be hiring an entry-level news reporter. I wanted that job, and he stopped me after class to suggest I apply. He said I had a good probability of getting it, that he'd write a reference for me. I wanted to surprise you with my news."

"And I surprised you with my proposal before you could."

"You did. You knew how much I wanted to be an on-camera newsperson. I'd thought you'd understand my hasty response once I told you about the possible job in Chicago. But you cut me short before I could tell you the details." She bit her lip. "You still had two years of seminary. I'd figured I could get some work experience before we got that serious. When you didn't seem to understand, I was confused and frustrated. You'd always understood before when no one else did."

Connor's guard went up. What had she expected?

She'd refused his proposal. He hadn't been in the most understanding of moods.

"I was afraid. The future with you that flashed in my head had me tied down in some small town just like Paradox Lake. I wanted something different, more."

"So you told me we needed a clean break," he ventured, "that you had better things to do than to be a small-town pastor's wife." His words tasted as bitter as they sounded.

"I'm so sorry. I wanted to hurt you as much as it hurt me when you didn't want to hear about the opportunity I thought the Chicago job would be."

And she had. He stared at the attic wall behind her.

"I didn't return your calls when I got back because part of me was afraid I'd give in to you and miss out on the opportunity."

And he avoided seeing Natalie in person because he hadn't wanted to risk her rejecting him again because he wasn't good enough. Connor realized that their breakup hadn't been entirely one-sided. He'd still had issues about being Jerry Donnelly's son that he hadn't worked out. He'd fallen back on his old defense of closing down, depending only on himself.

She shook her head. "It probably wouldn't have made a difference. My family wasn't as encouraging about the job in Chicago as I wanted, either. I thought you were all against me. I wanted to prove you all wrong. I know now that Mom and Dad were reserved about it because they didn't want me to be too disappointed if I didn't get the job. Kirk seemed to be the only person who had faith in me."

"Was that the only part he played?" Connor couldn't stop himself from asking, and he wanted to put part of the blame on something other than both of them being childish.

Her eyes widened.

Connor shifted on the hard wooden floor. "Jared said he'd read something in one of the suburban Chicago newspapers when he was racing in the Midwest."

She hugged herself. "I promise, I wasn't… There was nothing between Kirk and me, except a bad case of hero worship on my part, until I took the job in Chicago. But what Jared told you is probably true. I'm ashamed of my behavior, even though I thought he was divorced, and accept the reputation it gave me." Her voice caught. "The station director at the next station I worked at after Chicago didn't hire me for my reporting ability, if you know what I mean."

Compassion for Natalie smashed what was left of the wall shielding his heart. He wrapped his arms around her, and she rested her head on his chest, seemingly oblivious to the rustling Connor heard below them. He should release her, but couldn't.

The trapdoor dropped open. "Here they are." Natalie's niece's lilting voice carried through the attic. "I told you I thought I saw them come up here."

Natalie jerked away from him as if burned, and Connor looked down into the faces of most of the members of the Hazardtown Community Church women's group and evangelism committee.

Horror filled Natalie. She glanced from Connor to the faces below to her niece, who was sneaking away down the hall. "Amelia Theresa Bissette. Stay right there."

Natalie scrambled down the ladder ahead of Connor.

The women parted, giving her free access to Amelia. "What were you thinking?"

"What do you mean, Aunt Natalie?" Amelia said, eyes wide with feigned innocence.

Sympathy for her sister crashed over Natalie. Andie had to deal with this—times two—every day.

"She means, why did you lie to us and trap us in the attic?"

Natalie started at the deep boom of Connor's voice, her heart leaping to her throat before sinking. She could handle her nieces. He didn't need to come to her rescue. The last time she'd let a man intervene for her had been the start of the mess she was in—Kirk and his job offer in Chicago. Natalie straightened to her full five foot five. She knew Connor well enough still to know he didn't have any ulterior motives. Maybe worse, he felt sorry for her, for the situation she'd gotten herself in with Kirk. She didn't need anyone's sympathy. Why hadn't she stuck to her plan not to tell anyone the real reasons she came home for Christmas this year? Now, she'd told Connor about being out of work *and* the fiasco with Kirk.

Connor cleared his throat, waiting for Amelia.

She knew why. Because he was Connor. He'd always been so easy to talk to.

Amelia looked up at him wide-eyed. "Aimee and I didn't mean anything. Don't be mad, Pastor Connor. We really like you."

Her niece batted her eyelashes. *She batted her eyelashes.* Andie and Rob were in for some interesting times ahead.

"And Aimee and I really like Aunt Natalie." Amelia beamed at her.

"I like your aunt, too," Connor said.

Natalie couldn't allow herself to dissect his meaning, even if she wanted to. She had to stop this train wreck of a conversation. "Where is Aimee?" Natalie made a show of checking the time on her phone. "We probably should get going."

"But Pastor Connor asked me a question. It would be rude to not answer him."

Connor lifted an eyebrow. Normally, Natalie would agree with her niece.

"Anyway," Amelia continued, "everyone at church says it's time Pastor Connor thought about getting married."

Connor cringed.

"And Mom was telling Dad that she wouldn't be surprised if you were out of here in a flash as soon as Grandma is better."

Natalie's stomach churned. She would be if she had any place to go.

Amelia tipped her face up at Natalie. "We don't want you to leave."

Her niece's words planted a seed of belonging inside her.

"Mom's getting impossible. She won't even let us wear makeup to school. There's no talking to her."

The twins were going to be sorely disappointed if they thought she'd be able to sway her older sister, or interfere with Andie and Rob's parenting for that matter.

"We figure, if you stay here, we'll have somebody to talk to. You can give us pointers. You used to have to live with her. She tries to boss you around like she bosses us."

Connor's mouth twitched. If he lost it, she would, too. An awareness of the church women standing behind them pinched her already jangled nerves. Bursting into laughter was not an appropriate reaction to the situation.

"Answer Pastor Connor's question."

"All right," Amelia huffed as if she was really being put upon. "Mom said you and Pastor Connor used to go out before you let him get away."

Natalie tapped her foot and avoided Connor's gaze.

"If you two could start going out again, maybe you'd want to stick around for a while, and make Aimee and my lives easier. You wouldn't have to get married or anything."

Natalie and Connor shook their heads in unison.

"Or would you have to?" Amelia blurted before Natalie could say anything. "Our friend Norah lent us one of her mother's romance novels. The vicar had to marry the woman he rescued from a snowstorm because he brought her back to his house, and they were there all day by themselves until his housekeeper came back from her day off."

Natalie tensed at the muffled laughs behind them.

"No, we don't have to get married," Connor said, using a tone so stern it left Amelia's mouth hanging open.

While Natalie was appreciative of his support, did his denial have to be quite so strenuous? Her throat clogged. She shouldn't have let down her guard and told him so much.

"Hey, what's going on up here?" Natalie's friend Autumn asked as she and Aimee reached the top step. "We got back from picking up the extra fir boughs and no one was downstairs."

The hall went silent for a moment before Connor took

charge. "Amelia couldn't find Hope. Natalie and I both had the idea she might be in the attic."

Autumn's gaze moved from Connor and Natalie to the group of women behind them. "Did you find her?" she asked, her voice rising in alarm.

"Hope's in her room sleeping," Aimee said.

Aimee squirmed under Natalie's glare. Her hunch was right. The twins were in on this together. "Amelia, Aimee, get your things. We're leaving."

"But the decorating isn't done," Aimee said as she exchanged a glance with her twin.

Amelia's answering shrug of wide-eyed innocence, as if she had no idea why her aunt had said that, fried Natalie's temper. "Your decorating is done. Downstairs." What had happened to the sweet little girls she used to babysit when she was in high school and home on college breaks? She hardly knew these two. Her throat constricted. But that was her fault. She'd hardly been home in the past five years to get to know them.

The twins shuffled by Autumn and down the stairs.

"We'd better get back to work," Karen Hill said. The women followed the twins with Autumn giving Natalie a questioning look before turning to go downstairs. A sharp longing for the time when she and Autumn and a third friend, Jules Hill, had shared everything pierced her. But she'd let those friendships go, too.

"I'm going to check on Hope." Connor touched her arm. "It's okay. This will blow over." He motioned to the stairs and the ominous level of chatter. "They're good Christian women. They won't make anything more of it than it was. A prank by your mischievous nieces."

She gave him a weak smile and watched him duck into his little sister's room. But nothing was okay, and it might never be. Worse, she felt she'd brought her dirt home with her and it was rubbing off on Connor.

Connor looked down at Hope, who was fast asleep. He gently pulled her thumb from her mouth. She moved her lips and stilled. Hope looked so much like Jared, he could almost understand why a few local people believed she was his brother's illegitimate daughter—almost, except that those beliefs were rooted in jealousy and vindictiveness. In actuality, she resembled their father in pictures taken before alcohol had decimated his looks.

He'd been the only one of the three of them who'd ever considered having kids. Josh still said he didn't want any. Jared had gotten a ready-made family when he married Becca. Connor might have offered to take Hope if Jared hadn't married. He'd grown to love Hope more as a father than as a brother when she'd lived with him and Jared at the parsonage last year. But she was better off as part of Jared and Becca's family, where she had both father and mother figures. Things might have been different if he was married. If… A picture of Natalie flashed in his mind, the old Natalie, caroling with her college church group at a nursing home.

No. He wasn't going to go there.

"She's a sweetheart," Karen Hill said from the doorway behind him. "Are you okay?"

"Sure. I was just checking on her. I can't believe she slept through…you know." He jerked his head toward the hall behind Karen. "I shouldn't have let her stay up so late and get so tired."

Karen came and stood by him beside Hope's bed. "Don't blame yourself."

But he did, for more than letting Hope wheedle him into watching one more *Veggie Tales* DVD.

"Some kids are like that. One minute they're racing around, the next they're out like a light. Jack was like that. One time I sent him to the basement to take laundry out of the dryer. He took forever, so I went down and there he was fast asleep on the cold cement floor." She looked at Hope, then him. "But Hope isn't really what's bothering you."

"I'm fine." He stared at the throw rug on the floor by the bed. Gram had made it from old socks.

"There'll be some talk. It's inevitable. But it'll pass soon. No harm to you."

Connor faced Karen. She'd been his Sunday school teacher and youth group leader with her husband. She'd helped him more than once when he was a teen by listening to him. His brothers always made him feel girlie when he wanted to talk things out. And Mom had more than enough with work and Dad. He hadn't wanted to lay anything else on her.

"It's not me I'm worried about."

"Natalie? Nothing fazes Natalie." Karen waved him off.

That was the old Natalie, not the brittle shadow of her former self he'd seen at pageant practice and today. "She's not the same as she was when she left Paradox Lake. She's been…through some things." He wished he could tell Karen. But that would be betraying both Natalie and his ministry.

"Terry hasn't said anything, except how glad she was that Natalie came home. Is she okay?"

"I don't know," he said truthfully. "And Natalie may

not have spoken with her mother." But she'd talked with him. His heart swelled.

Karen arched her eyebrow. "I'll do my best to keep what happened this afternoon the innocent incident it was. For both your sakes."

"I'd appreciate that."

"We have a good group downstairs. It shouldn't be a problem."

Connor hoped not. He was having enough trouble dealing with Natalie's return, even if it was temporary— or, maybe, because it was temporary—without them being the center of local gossip. "There's tea, coffee and hot chocolate in the cupboard above the stove," he said. "Would you mind seeing what everyone wants and getting things started? Gram sent over some Christmas cookies, too. I'll be down in a minute." *After I'm sure Natalie has left.*

The twins chattered all the way home. As far as Natalie could tell, neither felt any remorse for the situation they'd put her and Connor in. Remembering how comforted she'd felt in Connor's arms, she couldn't say she did, either. Not right now. But she was sure she would later.

Natalie pulled her mother's car into Andie and Rob's driveway and the girls had their doors open almost before she'd stopped.

"Thanks for the ride, Aunt Natalie," they called, dashing to the door.

They weren't going to get off that easy. Did they really think she wouldn't say anything to their parents? Natalie turned off the car and trudged through the snow to the house.

"Hi." Andie held the door open for her. "I thought you might stop in."

Had someone already called and told Andie what the twins had done?

"Come on in the kitchen and sit down. I figured Mom would want you to get all the details about Robbie."

"How is he?" Natalie swallowed her guilt. She'd been so caught up in her own feelings she'd forgotten all about her nephew. "Mom told me she was going to call you."

"I didn't check the voice mail. Robbie is okay. I ended up taking him to urgent care. It's some kind of bug that's going around."

"Not the flu?" Natalie asked.

"No."

"That's a relief."

"It sure is. But I'll have to keep him home from preschool for a few days. I was wondering if you could you watch him Thursday afternoon? I'm scheduled to work some extra hours."

The real reason Andie had flagged her in. She couldn't help wondering what her sister would have done if she wasn't here.

"That is, if Mom doesn't need you. It would only be from one until a little after three when Aimee and Amelia get home from school. Rob will be around doing chores so the girls will be fine watching him then. We could really use the money for Christmas."

Shame flooded Natalie. "Sure. Mom thinks I'm doing too much for her anyway."

Andie laughed. "You know how Mom is. Anything is too much."

She shouldn't be so sensitive, but her sister's dismissive comment hurt. "I did get Mom to sit down the other morning and take a short nap today." It was hard to keep a defensive tone out of her voice.

Andie looked past Natalie to the kitchen doorway. "Did you girls need something?"

"I think they were listening to see if I was telling you what they did this afternoon," Natalie answered for her nieces.

"What now?" Exasperation colored Andie's face. "Aimee and Amelia, get in here."

Her sister's tone was almost enough to make Natalie feel sorry for the twins. But not quite.

"What did they do?"

When Natalie told her about the twins trapping her and Connor in the attic, it sounded almost humorous. Maybe people would see it that way.

"You lied and put your aunt and Pastor Connor in an uncomfortable situation. Go to your room until dinner, and you won't be going to Monica's birthday sleepover on Friday."

"But Mom, we apologized. And Pastor Connor said they wouldn't have to get married or anything," Aimee protested.

"Married! Where did that come from?" Andie asked.

"Apparently from a Regency romance one of their friends lent them," Natalie explained.

"It was a Christian romance," Amelia said.

Natalie bit her lip to stop herself from smiling.

"Everyone says Pastor Connor should get married," Amelia said. "Even you, Mom. We heard you tell Dad so, and that Pastor Connor and Aunt Natalie used to go out. You said Aunt Natalie seemed to be getting her act together and maybe she'd know a good thing when she saw it now."

Andie winced and all the humor Natalie had felt disappeared. She'd always known Connor was a good thing. That was all the more reason she didn't need her nieces, sister or anyone else pushing her and Connor together. He deserved better.

Andie raised her hands, fingers spread. "Enough. Go to your room."

The twins stomped out.

"Sorry about that," Andie said. "I've been a mother long enough to know I should watch what I say when little ears may be listening."

That was it? No apology for what she'd said, only regrets that the twins had heard it?

"I don't know what gets into those two. I can't understand them," Andie said.

"Don't be too hard on yourself," Natalie said. "The preteen years aren't easy ages for girls or their mothers."

"No." Andie shook her head. "They're like you. They do whatever pops in their heads without thinking about how their actions might affect others. I couldn't understand how you could do half the things you've done to Mom, nor do I understand the twins' actions. I'm working on them to be sure the worst doesn't happen."

But she was a lost cause? Natalie swallowed. "That's what you think of me?"

"Honestly? I don't mean to hurt you, but kind of. You dumped Connor and rushed off to Chicago to take that job. And how long did you stay there before you were off to a different job and then another?"

"It's called building a career," Natalie countered. Or in her case, trying to hang on to one.

"And is being too busy to come home and see Mom and Dad part of building a career, too?"

Natalie pushed away from the table. "No, that was finances. Living in the Chicago area was—is—expensive."

The way Andie's eyes narrowed when she corrected *was* to *is* made Natalie's throat constrict. Andie didn't need to know she'd lost her job. She stood. "I'm going to go now. I can't do this."

"Neither can I. I don't have time for your drama."

"Fine, I'll stay—" The weary look in her sister's eyes stopped Natalie from finishing with "out of your way." "I'll stay with Robbie on Thursday. I'm sure Mom will be okay with it."

"Only if you want to," Andie said, "and for the record, you're probably still too selfish to appreciate a good man like Connor."

Pain banded her chest. Andie had to get the last word. No, she wasn't too selfish to appreciate it. She could appreciate it all too well. Nor was she foolish enough to pursue the attraction to him she still felt, no matter how much her memories were pushing her to.

Chapter Five

Connor paced the front of the conference center auditorium, silently practicing his words as he often did with his sermons.

He'd texted Natalie and asked her to meet with him forty-five minutes before the pageant choir practice to work out a way to choose the soloists for "O Holy Night." Before her surgery, Natalie's mother, Terry, had found an arrangement that had male and female solo parts. Today, Terry had emailed him the names of potential soloists she and the choir directors of the other participating churches had put together.

He'd wondered why she was sending him the list instead of giving it to Natalie. Then he'd seen Natalie's name at the top of the list. Even before he read Terry's note, Connor knew that as the pageant's music director, Natalie would never put herself out in the competition for the women's solo.

But choosing soloists wasn't what had him pacing, even though he expected some rivalry among the participants from the various congregations. It was his guilty conscience for hiding out upstairs on Sunday and leaving Natalie to face the church women alone. Alone, except for her devious nieces. He'd thought about calling her yesterday, but hadn't.

"Hi."

Natalie's greeting stopped his pacing. He watched her walk down the aisle toward him. "Hey, how are you doing?"

"Okay." She placed her folder of music on the piano bench.

"I mean. You know. Sunday." Not exactly the compassionate inquiry he'd practiced.

She placed her hands on her hips. "I've got Aimee, Amelia *and* Andie mad at me. But I guess that's to be expected."

He leaned his hip against the side of the piano, as casually as he could with his nerves playing racquetball against each other.

"Andie grounded the girls, so they can't go to their friend's sleepover birthday party this weekend. And Andie…" Natalie shook her head. "It doesn't matter."

He'd been worried about the church women talking. He hadn't thought about her family giving her grief. "I'm sorry."

"It's not your fault. Unless you put the twins up to it."

"No." His voice echoed in the empty auditorium.

"Paul suggested it." The corner of her mouth twitched before her mouth spread into a wide grin. "Just thought I'd check."

He relaxed. This was the Natalie he used to know.

"Paul thought it was hysterical."

"It is kind of funny when you think about it," Connor said. Although amused wasn't the way he'd felt when he was holding Natalie, or when the trapdoor dropped open.

"Yeah, funny when you're not living it."

He straightened. "You are okay? No one's said anything to you?"

"I haven't been anywhere, except here, since Sunday." Her eyes narrowed and she lifted her chin. "Has someone said something to you? I'm the one who should apologize for causing you trouble. Aimee and Amelia were with me."

Way to go, Donnelly. Just when she was lightening up. "No one's said anything to me."

Natalie glanced back at the clock over the auditorium doors. "We'd better get started. People will be arriving soon."

"Right."

"How did you want to do this?" she asked.

Connor shrugged. "Have people audition and you can pick the best two."

Natalie rubbed the toe of her boot against the leg of the piano bench. "I'm not comfortable having the final say. I thought it might be fun to do it like one of the talent reality shows. I hate to admit it, but they've become one of my weaknesses."

The only reality show he'd ever seen was *The Amazing Race.* "Sure, why not."

"Good." A slow smile spread across her face. "I wasn't sure you'd agree. So, anyone who wants to can try out, and when the last person finishes, the choir can vote."

"Your mother sent me a list of people recommended by the choir directors at the participating churches."

"She gave me the list, too."

Not likely the same one she'd given him with Natalie's name front and center.

"I'd like to open it up to anyone who's interested, unless you have some reason we shouldn't," Natalie said.

"Time's the only reason I can think of. We can't afford to have the entire practice used up with tryouts."

Natalie pushed her hair behind her ears. She'd worn it down tonight, softly curling on her shoulders, rather than having it pulled back or pinned up as she had the other times he'd seen her lately. It was a little shorter than she'd worn it in college, but still as soft. Or so it had seemed when a stray stand had brushed against his cheek when she'd rested her head on his shoulder Sunday in the attic.

"From what Mom told me, that shouldn't be a problem. She said she often has to prod people into taking solo or duet parts. Hence the list. She also suggested that you and I sing the parts for the choir so those trying out for solos have a feel for the arrangement."

"Everyone should know 'O Holy Night.' Wouldn't the song sheets and your playing it be enough?"

"Maybe not. Mom pointed out that she's known some wonderful singers who don't read music well. They sing by ear."

"Excuse me." One of the choir members from another church approached Natalie.

Connor had been so focused on Natalie, enjoying her enthusiasm for her reality show tryouts idea, that he hadn't heard the woman come in. "Hi, we haven't met. I'm Connor Donnelly, pastor at Hazardtown Community Church."

The woman introduced herself to Connor and Natalie and addressed Natalie. "At the last practice you said if we weren't sure of our voice range, we could see you before this one."

"Sure." Natalie favored her with a warm smile that lit Natalie's eyes with a well-remembered glow he hadn't seen since she'd returned. "Let me give Connor this music sheet, and we'll do a quick test."

"I sang soprano in my high school chorus, but that was a while ago." The woman glanced from Natalie to Connor.

"I'll just take this—" he lifted the sheet music he'd rolled into a tube "—and study it in the back." He waved the cylinder toward the door. The woman seemed as anxious to sing in front of him as he was to sing in front of the choir. Not that his singing would clear the room. But Jared was the one who'd inherited a singing voice from their mother. He walked up the aisle and took a seat in the last row by the door.

"Hey." Jared stepped through the door ahead of several other choir members. "I see you're taking my advice."

"How's that?"

Jared waited until the others passed. "Keeping your distance from Natalie. But this may be a little extreme." With a laugh, he motioned between Connor and Natalie.

"Lay off. I'm giving them some privacy."

Natalie ran through the music scale with the woman singing "Do, re, mi…" and then starting over an octave higher. Jared slid into the seat ahead of him.

"I'm supposed to be reviewing this music." Connor tapped his knee with the paper tube. "Natalie wants us to sing the solo parts for everyone before we start tryouts."

He waited to see if Jared would volunteer. He was big on trying to come to his brothers' rescue. When he didn't, Connor considered asking him. He unrolled the music. *No.* He had to man up and face singing with Natalie publicly, as he'd done with her countless times in private. Learn to face that challenge *and* work more closely with her without wanting to turn back the hands of time.

When Natalie finished running through the scales with the choir member, she glanced past the people walking toward her to the back of the auditorium, where Connor sat talking with his brother. Connor scowled at Jared. Why had she agreed with her mother that she and Connor singing "O Holy Night" together for the choir would be a good idea? Because she'd thought it would be fun. She hadn't even given him the opportunity to agree. Or, more likely, to disagree, given his expression and the contrast between the casual way Jared leaned over his seat and the rigid way Connor held himself.

A hand appeared in front of her face, breaking her line of vision.

"They do make a gawk-worthy sight, don't they?" her friend Autumn asked.

"What? I was thinking."

Autumn smiled. "Let me guess about what."

"Music, actually."

Autumn put her hands on her hips and cocked her head to the side.

"We need to have tryouts for the two pageant solos tonight. Mom suggested Connor and I sing the parts so everyone can hear the arrangement. It didn't occur to me he wouldn't want to." She looked back at the guys again.

"I'm saying this as a friend. The time's past when Connor will do something he doesn't want to do just to please you, or anyone else, unless it's for the good of his congregation or he believes God wants him to take that action."

Natalie bit her lip. Her admiration for Connor grew. She could remember too many times when she'd wheedled Connor into doing things he hadn't wanted to do.

Autumn didn't wait for her to respond. "Also, as a friend, I was wondering if you want to stop by my house on your way home tonight to catch up. As I was leaving, Jon got called into the birthing center. I have a plate of Christmas cookies Gram dropped off last night when I was out at a home birth."

"The snickerdoodle ones I loved when we were kids?" Natalie asked.

"The very ones."

"I'll be there."

As with Connor's seemingly easy acceptance of her, Natalie couldn't express how much Autumn's simple invitation meant after the way she'd let their friendship drop. Nor was this the time or place to. Add one more item on her "make things right with family and friends" list.

"Let's get this practice going." Natalie raised her hand to Connor, who was now standing in the back of the auditorium greeting the last couple of choir members straggling in.

He acknowledged her signal with a broad smile that made her question whether she'd imagined his resistance to singing with her. She watched him close the doors and stride down to the stage area.

"I'd better go take my place in the choir," Autumn said.

"Right." Natalie had forgotten that Autumn was still standing next to her. She steeled herself. She couldn't let the nostalgia of earlier times color reality. She and Connor were different people than they'd been five years ago.

"Listen up," Connor said, stepping into the spot where

Autumn had been. "Did everyone get my email saying we're holding tryouts for the solo parts tonight?"

A murmur of agreement flowed across the stage.

"Okay. Natalie will explain the process."

"I thought it would be fun to handle the tryouts something like a reality show." Natalie ignored the groans from a couple of the choir members. "Connor and I will sing the parts so you can hear the arrangement. Then everyone who wants to try out will have a practice sing and a final sing. If you're happy with your first pass, you can forego the second one. Once all the contestants have finished their tryouts, you all will choose our soloists. Any ques—"

"Sorry."

Natalie spun around to see Andie rushing down the aisle. What was she doing here? Andie had told their mother she was too busy to sing in the pageant this year. Natalie thought it was more because she was the choir director.

"I was sure Natalie said practice was at seven." Leave it to her sister to lay the blame on her.

"No matter," Connor said. "Everyone's welcome, on time or not. Take your place on the stage. There's a spot next to Karen. Natalie just finished explaining how we're going to choose the soloists for 'O Holy Night.' You'll see once we start."

Natalie waited until Andie was in place on the stage. *Some things never changed.* As unsisterly as it was, she couldn't shake the thought that Andie had joined the choir purposely to undermine her. "Ready?" she asked Connor. He nodded, and she played the song through once before beginning the first verse.

He joined her on "O night divine" and went into the

second verse. She closed her eyes and gave in to the music, his voice taking her back to her junior year of college, before Connor had come to Syracuse for seminary. Warm remembrances filled her. He'd driven from Houghton College for the weekend, and she'd talked him in to coming with her college Christian group to sing at a local nursing home. Afterward, he'd talked with several of the home's residents and led them in a prayer for a joyous Christmas. They'd walked hand-in-hand under a canopy of stars in the crisp night air to her dorm. Suddenly conscious of him standing only inches away, Natalie could almost feel the soft good-night kiss they'd shared before he'd headed over to another building to stay with one of her friends from the group.

Natalie fumbled a note and almost missed joining Connor in the last three lines of his verse, leading into her solo of the last verse. She put all her concentration into finishing the hymn and breathed a sigh of relief when she played the last note, anxious for him to take his place with the choir to put the distance between them.

Someone clapped, sending the choir into a round of applause.

"Thanks," Connor said when it quieted. "So, who's game? Remember, I have this list." He pulled a folded sheet of paper from his pocket and waved it at the choir.

A couple of women raised their hands. Natalie's heart sunk when she saw Andie was one of them. No, it might be good if Andie got the part. Working together could help them mend their relationship.

"Come on, guys," Connor prompted when none of the men volunteered. "Do I have to exercise executive privilege? Jared, you're on the list."

"Sorry, bro, the part's for a tenor. I'm a baritone."

"You heard Natalie. She said she can adjust the arrangement."

Natalie smiled at their banter. She should reach out to Andie. Maybe she and Andie and Claire could go Christmas shopping together or something.

"Ken?" Connor addressed a choir member from his church.

"Sorry, I can't make the commitment. You wouldn't want to be left high and dry if I was a no-show the night of the pageant because I got an emergency call to make a fuel oil delivery or go fix someone's furnace. But I have a suggestion."

Connor relaxed his stance. Or at least it looked that way to Natalie.

"I think you should do the solo," Ken said.

Natalie shot Connor a sympathetic look as the men of the choir in particular drowned out his protest. He couldn't be any more anxious to work closer together than she was.

"We'll see. Maybe one of you guys will muster enough guts after you hear the women try out. Go ahead, Natalie."

She ran through the tryouts, not feeling the least bit guilty for possibly putting slightly more into Andie's accompaniment. Not that she needed it. Her sister clearly outsang the other two women. When Andie finished her second round, Natalie gave her a thumbs-up behind the piano, where the others couldn't see it. Andie nodded.

Natalie glanced over at Connor and caught him gazing at her raised thumb. Heat flooded her face. She shouldn't be displaying favoritism, but Connor and Andie would be perfect vocalists for the hymn.

"Thank you, ladies," he said as Andie returned to the

choir. "That was beautiful. Men, do I have a volunteer or two now?"

"No, let's go ahead and vote," a male voice called from the back.

Connor turned to Natalie as if not sure how to proceed.

Natalie pushed back from the piano and stood. "I have papers and pens, if I could have a couple people help pass them out and collect the votes. Write your vote for the female part from the three women we just heard and, I guess, anyone you want for the male part."

Connor's expression plainly said "Thanks a lot."

She shrugged. What else could she do if they were to get any practice time in tonight?

The ballots were quickly distributed and collected. Natalie split them between Connor and her to count. A noose formed around her stomach after the first few ballots and pulled tighter with each additional one. She finished hers first to catch Connor's mouth draw to a grim line. "Mine are almost all for you and me," she said for Connor's ears only.

"The same here." Connor called down two people from other churches and explained what had happened. A buzz of conversation filled the room as the others recounted the ballots.

"Congratulations," one of the recounters said when they'd finished. "Want me to make the announcement?"

"Please," Natalie squeaked out ahead of Connor.

"After an impartial recount," the man said, "the winners are Natalie and Pastor Connor."

During the brief pause before the choir exploded in applause, Natalie sought out Andie, hoping to wordlessly convey her feelings about the vote. Andie's face was a study in neutrality. The knot strangling her stomach pulled an inch tighter.

Natalie finished the practice as if on autopilot, avoiding eye contact with everyone. She mechanically accepted the congratulations of the choir members, keeping a watch for her sister. Somehow Andie slipped by. As the room emptied to Connor and her, she quickly gathered her things. Too quickly. The sheet music slipped from her grasp. Watching the pages fall to the floor, Natalie silently implored, *Lord, I know You're trying to teach me something, but could You give me a little clue what?* She sensed Connor moving to help her. *And how I'm supposed to harness my old feelings and work together with Connor as if they don't exist. You know I couldn't bear to fail him again.*

Connor's hand brushed hers as they gathered the pages. She disguised her sharp intake of breath with a little cough that seemed to resound in the empty auditorium.

He tapped the short edge of the papers he'd picked up on the floor to straighten the stack. "Here you go."

"Thanks." She added them to hers and placed them in the folder.

Connor rose, offering her a hand up.

She swallowed. She couldn't ignore his offer. Nor could she ignore the spark his simply brushing her hand had caused. Natalie took his hand, letting go as quickly as she could without being obvious. A light flickered in his eyes. So much for not showing her feelings.

"Interesting night," he said.

"You've got that right," she agreed.

He tucked his hands in the front pockets of his jeans.

"We couldn't have handled it any other way, not after giving the choir members the final vote."

Was that a dig? The choir voting on the "contestants" had been her idea. Natalie turned and closed the piano. "I guess not. Sorry I talked you into singing with me. You've got enough to do without being a soloist besides."

Connor smiled. "Who's to say they wouldn't have voted me in anyway, figuring I couldn't say no."

Natalie faced him. "People do that?"

"Yes, people have expectations."

"And you don't feel taken advantage of?" Natalie couldn't say she wouldn't.

"Not really. It works the other way when I need church volunteers. If I run out of different people to ask, I know I have some members who won't say no." The faint laugh lines at the corners of his eyes deepened. "Besides, in this case, being volunteered may be fun, give us a chance to get to know each other again."

Connor's casual words woke a yearning in Natalie she couldn't define, only that she couldn't have whatever it was. She reached for her coat on the chair next to the piano, avoiding his gaze so he couldn't see how his friendly words had affected her.

Connor beat her to it, holding the garment so she could slide her arms in. "We're going to need to get together to practice a couple of times," he said. "I'd rather not use the little time the choir has to practice."

Even though her head knew Connor was speaking as the pageant director, that his words didn't mean he wanted to spend time with her, Natalie's traitorous heart skipped a beat. "I'm sure Mom and Dad wouldn't mind us practicing at their house." *Where we wouldn't be alone.* "In fact, Mom might enjoy it."

"Okay, why don't we head over to the general store and catch a cup of coffee…or hot chocolate and see what dates work. I have my calendar on my phone."

Was Connor as anxious not to be alone with her as she was with him? She tamped down the feeling of giddiness that thought invoked. If he was, it couldn't be for the same reason she was.

"Sorry, I can't. I told Autumn I'd stop by on my way home. She said her grandmother had dropped off some Christmas cookies she needed help with."

"I've had Mrs. Hazard's cookies. No contest."

"Why don't you come, too?" she blurted. "It would be like old times. I'm sure Autumn won't mind." She and Connor had often done things with Autumn and her high school boyfriend, Jack. But they weren't in high school anymore, and she hadn't really been a friend to either Autumn or Connor in years.

"No, you and Autumn don't need me butting in. But you could smuggle out a few of Mrs. Hazard's cookies for me."

Natalie bit her tongue to suppress her jumbled emotions so she didn't say what she was feeling. *I miss you. I'm sorry. I wish we could go back.* "I'll see what I can do."

Chapter Six

Connor whistled "O Holy Night" as he walked up the shoveled path to the Delacroix's two-story frame farm house Thursday evening. Candles in each of the double-hung windows lit his way, and the wreath on the front door added to the warm welcome he'd always felt here. A welcome he was less sure of tonight.

He'd gotten only an "okay" text from Natalie in answer to the voice mail he'd left her asking whether tonight was a good time for them to get together and practice. Connor knocked on the door, remembering a time when he would have gone to the kitchen door and let himself in.

"Connor. What brings you here?" Paul asked as he swung the door open to let him in.

"Natalie and I are going to practice our solos for the pageant service." Or at least he thought they were. Maybe he should have followed up on her text.

"She's probably upstairs. Nat," he shouted loud enough to reach her anywhere in the old house, including the attic and basement. "Hand me your coat and sit down." Paul hung the coat on the doorknob to the front closet. "Claire and I are on our way out to find a combination birthday-Christmas gift for Renee. Our birthday is the twentieth. I need to have something in the mail by Saturday to make sure it gets to Haiti in time. It's the first birthday we've spent apart."

"How's she doing?" Connor asked, taking a seat in the living room and crossing his ankle over his knee. "I haven't had an email from her in a while."

"Still loving the work. She's talking about getting her masters in social work when she comes home."

"Hey, Connor," Claire said from the stairway. "Looking for Natalie? I think she's downstairs doing laundry."

Connor uncrossed his legs, more convinced he'd misread the meaning of Nat's text, or that she'd meant to send it to someone else.

"Want me to get her?" Claire asked.

"I called her," Paul said.

Claire made a face. "She probably didn't hear you over the dryer. I'll go." Claire disappeared into the back of the house and returned a minute later. "She'll be right up."

"You ready, then?" Paul asked Claire.

"Yep. See you, Connor."

"Later." Connor stared across the now-empty room at the Delacroix Christmas tree, drawn to the star on top. Its white blinking light made him wonder what Natalie had done with the one he'd bought her for the tree at her Syracuse apartment. He would have thrown it in the trash. She'd probably given it to a thrift shop or shelter.

"Pretty, isn't it?"

"Nat. I was beginning to think I'd gotten my information scrambled and we weren't practicing tonight."

"No, we are. Time got away from me. I told Mom I'd do the laundry when I got back from watching Robbie. Andie had a chance to pick up some extra hours at work. I'd forgotten how much laundry Dad and Paul could generate."

Connor forced a laugh. He hadn't intended to put her on the defensive. She stared at the tree now, a soft look on her face. Remembering other happy Christmases? Maybe she hadn't taken his words that way at all. He blew out a breath. He was overthinking.

"Where are Paul and Claire?" Natalie said, glancing around the room as if she'd just noticed they were alone. "Claire said you were all up here talking."

"Off shopping for a gift for Renee."

"Oh, Claire didn't say anything about that. Paul usually gives one of us girls money and we shop for him."

"Good plan. I'm a proponent of gift cards myself, except for Hope. I don't mind toy shopping."

"You always... Never mind."

He guessed Natalie was going to say he always gave her gifts on her birthday and Christmas. A hollow space opened in his chest. Shopping for Natalie had been different. It had been worth all the effort to see her face light up, to show her he cared enough to shop for something special for her.

"Should we get started? Mom and Dad have a TV program on Hallmark they like to watch at nine. I have the music out on the piano." She waved toward the instrument.

She'd set a time limit. All business. But what had he expected? "Ready when you are." He rose from the chair.

Before they reached the piano, Natalie's parents walked in.

"Mom, Dad, you going to be our audience?"

"No," her mother said. "We're going to take *Mémé*

for a drive around the lake to see the Christmas lights. Didn't I tell you? You know how your grandmother likes seeing the lights."

Confusion spread across Natalie's face. "I don't think so."

Connor scuffed his toe on the rug. Everyone being in the dark about what the rest of the family was doing sounded more like his family when he was growing up than Natalie's, or what he used to know of her family.

"I'm not sure when we'll be back," Terry said. "Paul already has the DVR set to record *Thursday Night Football* and Claire has it set for something else, so, if we're not here by nine, can you turn on my program and keep track of what's going on? Maybe the two of you would like to watch it. I think you'd like it, Connor. It's about—"

"Terry," Natalie's father said. "Mom's waiting."

"Okay, just one more thing. I baked cookies for you guys. Mary Hazard gave me the recipe. I remember you saying how much you liked them, Natalie. They're snickerdoodles. Have you ever had them, Connor?"

Connor stifled a groan. Now he knew what was going on. Another setup to get him dating and married. But Terry setting him up with Natalie? He hadn't seen that coming, and from Natalie's blush, she hadn't, either.

"Yes, they're one of my favorites," he said.

"Then, you're all set. You can practice your music in peace, then have cookies and coffee or tea and watch some TV. Just like old times."

Except during the old times, Natalie's father had always made sure there were at least two other people in the room with them at all times. In fact, by the way he was looking from him to Natalie, Connor half expected

him to say he and Terry could take Natalie's grandmother to view the lights another time.

"Thanks. I appreciate it."

Natalie's mother gave her husband's arm a tug. "You
said we had to get going."

"Yeah." He frowned.

Connor waited for John to tell them to behave themselves.

"Have fun," Terry said as she closed the front door
behind them.

"I am so embarrassed," Natalie said.

"Don't be."

"But she was so obvious. What on earth is she thinking?"

*That we made a good couple once. Maybe we could
again.* Natalie's outrage at her mother's attempted matchmaking animated her features in a way he'd seen far too
infrequently since she'd been back. He stepped closer,
breathing in the fresh pine scent of the tree, mingled with
the light floral scent of Natalie's perfume or shampoo.
The star's flashing light highlighted the blue-black shine
of her hair, making his heart trip in harmony. "It seems
to be the bane of all us bachelor pastors," he said to bring
things back into perspective. He was here to practice for
the Christmas pageant, not to fixate on how beautiful
Natalie looked tonight.

"And Paul and Claire had to have been in on it, too.
I told you his going shopping was odd."

"Not Paul," Connor said, remembering her brother's
surprise when he'd opened the front door. "And I'm sure
they didn't clue your father in. The frown on his face
when he realized we were going to be here alone made
me think he was going to cancel their drive around the

lake to stay here and chaperone. Remember how he used to send Paul and Renee in to watch TV with us and tag along if we went outside?"

Natalie stared at him. "You're not mad?"

"No, your mother didn't mean any harm."

"I'll talk with her." Natalie backed up a couple of inches as if she'd just noticed how close they were standing. "Make sure she understands we're friends and nothing more." Her cell phone buzzed. She pulled it from her pocket and glanced at the screen. "I should take this."

Connor nodded and crossed the room to the piano to give her a little privacy.

"Yes, I'm interested," Natalie said. "At least until after the holidays. Sure, I could probably arrange that. Let me know what you find out."

She joined him at the piano. "Sorry. That was my agent."

"A job opportunity?"

"Possibly."

Connor had pushed the fact that Natalie was here temporarily from his mind. Her phone call brought that and her ambitions blazing back. She'd soon be gone again, and he wasn't looking for a holiday fling. Despite the old feelings he'd allowed to surface, he'd respect the "friend" boundary she'd set.

"We should start practicing. I'm sure you have other things you could be doing tonight."

Connor followed Natalie. Nothing he'd rather be doing than spending the evening with her. But he'd get over it. He had before.

"Mom, how could you?" Natalie challenged her mother when her parents returned.

"Terry, I told you it wouldn't work," her father said before making a beeline up the stairs.

So her father had been in on it, or had at least known what her mother was doing.

"Why don't we go into the kitchen and have some of those cookies I made." Natalie's mother glanced at the TV. "It looks like my program is a repeat tonight."

"The cookies are gone."

"You and Connor ate them all?"

"No, I gave them to him to take home when he left, right after we finished practicing."

Her mother pursed her lips. "So you're not going to give yourself a chance."

"Connor and I are good. As friends. We talked when the twins locked us in the attic."

"Those two are something else," her mother said.

"To put it mildly. I hope their escapade hasn't caused too much talk."

"Not much, except among the small number of parishioners who are always looking to find fault with people."

That wasn't much reassurance. "I don't want to cause any problems for Connor. The other night when I stopped over at Autumn's, she said his contract with the church is up for renewal soon."

"Connor will be fine. Claire is on the administrative council, and she hasn't heard anything but the usual in the way of complaints against him, only the ones all pastors get."

"I don't want to be the source of any new ones."

Her mother waved her off. "I'm glad you and Autumn got to catch up. Karen said Jules and her family will be visiting for New Year's. The three of you will be able to get together like old times."

Natalie rubbed a catch in the tip of her thumbnail. Except it wasn't old times, not with her girlfriends and certainly not with Connor. And there was no way to make it so. "That would be fun, if I'm still here."

"What happened?" Her mother's eyes narrowed. "You're not harming Connor's pastorate by being here. You don't have to run back to Chicago."

Natalie's heart constricted. Her mother thought her career was "running away"? Mom had always been her support. "Nothing happened, except my agent called with a possible job opportunity, back at the station I started with."

"Is that wise?"

Natalie breathed in and out. "Kirk isn't there anymore, if that's what you're asking. There's all new management that wants to add a good news segment, like I did at the last station I was with."

"Oh, I know you liked that work."

Not the resounding encouragement Natalie might have expected. "I did. This job isn't for certain. My agent called to see if I would be interested. I wasn't going to say anything to anyone yet. I don't even have an interview."

"You have to do what you have to do. I like having you here helping. But I'm starting to get around and should be able to manage by myself after the holidays."

Guilt trips weren't Mom's usual style. Nothing was the same anymore. She shook off her personal pity party. "Can we change the subject? I may not even get an interview."

"All right," her mother agreed.

"Has Andie said anything to you about my getting the pageant solo? At practice, I was sure she had it."

"No, why?" Her mother put her hands on her hips. "Are you girls at it again?"

She shook her head. *Not since Andie's jibe about me being too selfish to appreciate Connor.* "She seemed really down when I was over there this afternoon. And the other night Autumn told me I should talk with Andie. Then Robbie said something today that I didn't understand at first. He was rearranging the Nativity scene and said their Christmas baby was lost and wasn't coming anymore. I thought he meant the baby Jesus figurine. I told him Mommy would put it out on Christmas. He said, 'No, the baby isn't coming anymore and that makes Mommy cry.' Did Andie have another miscarriage?"

"Yes. This time, she hemorrhaged so Dr. Hanlon told her they shouldn't try again. She's taken it hard. You know she and Rob had wanted a big family and how thrilled she was to have Robbie after trying for so many years after the twins were born."

Tears pricked Natalie's eyes. Andie did love babies. "I wondered. She didn't seem herself at practice, either. I'd wanted to talk with her before she left, but she slipped out." Natalie knew all too well how life's disappointments could pile up. "Why didn't you tell me when Andie first found out she was pregnant? I could have prayed for her, put her and Rob on my church's prayer list."

"Andie wanted to wait until she was into her second trimester before she went public with the news."

Her throat clogged. But she was family, not public. Little Robbie knew. "Do you think some girl time might cheer her up? After talking with Autumn, I'd thought I might ask Andie and Claire if they wanted to have lunch and go shopping or something."

"Getting out and having fun would do both of you good. You could drive down to the Adirondack Folk School Holiday Fair in Lake Luzerne on Saturday. How about I treat for the lunch? Andie's been picking up as many extra hours as she can at the store to make up for the pay she lost when she was out sick, but I think they still may be a little strapped for the holidays."

Something we have in common. Natalie wished she could tell her mother that she would treat, but the credit she had left on her credit card would barely buy her own lunch.

The front door flew open, and Paul and Claire walked through, stomping the snow off their boots on the doormat.

"I could sure use something hot to drink and some of those cookies you made, Mom," Paul said. "Claire dragged me all over the place, and we ended up going back to the first store for Renee's gift."

Claire slipped her coat off. "Yeah, I dragged him all over. We went to a grand total of three stores."

"What did you get?" Natalie asked.

"A chicken charm for her bracelet that comes with a matching donation of a hen to a family in a developing nation," Claire answered.

"Perfect," Natalie said, feeling a little left out that they hadn't asked her to come along, even though she would have had to turn them down. She and Connor had already made plans to practice.

"So, who else is in for those cookies and tea?" Paul asked.

"There aren't any cookies left. I gave them to Connor," Natalie said.

"So it worked," Claire said.

From the glee in Claire's voice, Natalie half expected her sister to start clapping.

"What worked?" Paul asked.

Natalie wasn't sure whether the irritation in her brother's voice was because he wasn't in the know or because the cookies were gone. "Mom and Claire's attempt to set Connor and me up."

"Oh, yeah?" Paul's voice perked up. "Connor's all right."

Natalie closed her eyes and counted to three. "No, it didn't work. Connor and I are just friends."

"And Natalie may have a job offer back in Chicago," her mother added as if their plot's failure needed a justification.

"Congrats, sis," Paul said to the twin frowns that creased their mother's and Claire's faces.

"I may have an interview for a job."

"Then you and Connor aren't…?" Claire said.

"No, we're not."

"Too bad," Paul said.

The pain of what couldn't be warred with the frustration of wanting to shout "This is my life, stay out of it."

"You'd be okay if I tell Karen Hill to go ahead and try to fix Connor up with her daughter-in-law's sister?" her mother asked. "She said to ask you before she did."

Natalie stifled a groan. How did Connor put up with it? She wrapped her arms around herself. "He's a free agent. I have no hold on Connor."

The dark house that greeted him when he got home fit right in with Connor's mood. He glared at the structure. He always left the porch lights on, and he was sure he'd put the kitchen one on as well. He pulled down the garage door and made his way toward the door between the garage and the house. His toe kicked a box or something right before he reached the steps. Flashing his cell phone down at his foot, he saw it was one of the Christmas ornament boxes. The stray cat that had been hanging around, but he hadn't been able to catch, must have gotten in and knocked it out of the recycle bin. He juggled the container of cookies Natalie had given him, then scooped up the box and chucked it under his arm. It shouldn't have been out here anyway. He'd need it to store the ornaments when he took the tree down.

Connor let himself in, placed the cookie container on the kitchen counter and hit the light switch, which he found already flicked on. He tried the garage light. No go there, either. The power must be out. He looked across the backyard at the church building. The front light there was out, too. The ornament box rattled when he pulled it out from under his arm and placed it next to the cookie container. He should go out and fire up the generator so the well pump would work and he'd have some lights. And, if he wanted to stay warm, he needed to bring in some more wood for the woodstove insert in the living room fireplace. But his curiosity about what was in the box got the best of him.

He flipped it open and shined his cell phone on the contents. His breath hitched. Natalie had thrown out the star he'd bought for her tree in Syracuse—in his trash. No, anyone could have put it out there. But how did it get here in the first place? Didn't matter. He stepped on the pedal to open the kitchen trash can but couldn't let go of the ornament. Like he couldn't seem to let go of Natalie, despite the fact that she obviously wanted only friendship from him. He placed the star back in the box to give to the church consignment shop. Closing the lid, he prayed, *Lord, give me the strength to be professional enough and man enough to honor Natalie's wishes and get back on track with the life I had before she came back.*

A noise in the garage startled him from his prayer. The cat?

"Hey, bro, up for some company and pizza?" His brother Josh stepped into the kitchen.

The pungent scent of the flat box he held churned Connor's stomach. *Not really.* "Sure, come on in."

"Power's out at my apartment, too. I heard at the pizzeria that a transformer is down. The power company's not sure when they'll have it back up." Josh walked by him and placed the pizza on the table. "I thought you'd have the generator going. Something wrong with it? I'll take a look."

Connor gritted his teeth. He didn't need Josh to look at his generator. If something was wrong with it, he was perfectly capable of assessing the problem himself. Just because he hadn't worked as a mechanic like Jared or studied mechanical drawing like Josh didn't mean Connor couldn't repair things.

"I just got here myself. Natalie and I were practicing our solos." Connor dug in the counter drawer for a flashlight.

"Uh-huh, alone at the conference center? Hazard Cove Road doesn't have power, either."

"No, at her parents' house, and you can lose the innuendoes. Natalie and I are nothing more than friends, and that's all we'll ever be. She's made that perfectly clear," Connor added under his breath.

"Shot you down again, eh?"

Not enough under his breath. "I'm going out to turn on the generator and get some wood. You can give me a hand."

Josh opened the door and let Connor go first, which only served to increase his irritation. He grabbed the log carrier he kept in the garage next to the steps and led the way out the door with the flashlight.

"If Natalie is out of the picture, you might be interested to know that Jack Hill's sister-in-law, Brianne, is also back in town. She had a huge crush on you back when you were in school. There's no accounting for taste."

Connor plowed through the snow toward the generator. He remembered. It was about the time he and Natalie had started dating. Brianne had been a pain, following him around and giggling with her friends. "She was in seventh or eighth grade, and I was a junior."

Josh whistled. "I saw her at the pizzeria. She doesn't look anything like a seventh or eighth grader anymore."

Connor shoved the wood carrier at Josh. "Make yourself useful."

"What? If you're not interested, maybe I'll ask her out. Sounds like she's planning to stick around. She's taken a long-term substitute teaching job at the elementary school."

Unlike Natalie, who sounded like she was getting antsy to leave already. Connor turned the generator on and the house lit up. "What about Tessa?"

"What about her? We're friends. She knows I like to keep my options open."

Classic Josh. Connor swallowed his disgust and walked over to the woodpile to help him.

As they reentered the kitchen, Connor caught the

final ring of the house phone in the dining room. "Put the wood in the living room and start the fire, if you would. I need to check that call."

He punched in the number and got his voice mail. "Connor, it's Jack. Mom is making me do this. I owe her one. She wants me to set up a double date with Suzi and me, and her sister and you. Some craft thing in Lake Luzerne on Saturday. The women want to go. I'm good if you don't. Let me know."

Connor replaced the receiver. Maybe he should be like Josh, explore other options, actual options. It might loosen the hold Natalie had on him.

Chapter Seven

Natalie pulled her mother's car into a parking space in front of the Adirondack Folk School. "Wasn't this a great idea?" she asked, glancing at Andie in the passenger seat. She couldn't read her. Andie had accepted Natalie's invitation readily enough and had chatted about the kids and her job and her family's Christmas plans for the first few minutes of the drive. But she'd gotten more and more quiet the farther they drove from Paradox Lake.

"It was your idea," Andie said flatly.

"My idea was lunch. Mom suggested the fair. She said you and Claire had talked about going other years, but hadn't. Too bad Claire had to work today." Natalie shut off the car. It would have been good to have Claire as a bridge between her and Andie.

"I hope it's not too much for Mom having Robbie and the twins there," Andie said, making no motion to open her door.

Was that what was bothering Andie? "She'll be fine. She has Dad to help, and Paul said he'd take them sledding out back."

Andie clutched her purse. "He wouldn't let Robbie

go down the hill by himself, would he? Robbie might beg him to. He seems to think he can do anything the twins can do."

"I'm sure he wouldn't." Or, at least she hoped he wouldn't. She remembered Paul and Renee at the same age wanting to do everything she and her older siblings did.

Natalie got out of the car and waited for her sister in front of the white clapboard building. When Andie finally emerged from the vehicle, Natalie pressed the car lock.

"I've got this," Natalie said when they stepped up to the reception counter to pay their admissions. She palmed her mother's debit card so Andie wouldn't see it wasn't hers and tried to ignore her guilt about letting her sister think she was treating. She'd let Andie know that Mom was buying their lunch. Looking at the colorful festival flyer the woman at the counter had given her, Natalie asked, "Where do you want to start?"

Andie shrugged. "You pick."

"The jewelry might be fun. Maybe I'll find something for Aimee and Amelia."

Andie returned her smile with a pained look. Why couldn't she keep her mouth shut? Mom had said she thought Andie and Rob were short on cash for Christmas, and Andie was picking up extra work hours at the store. Andie probably thought she was rubbing it in that she could afford custom jewelry for the twins. Not that she could, unless she found something small, like earrings. What bothered her more, though, was that Andie wasn't responding like Andie.

Natalie glanced at the flyer again. "The blacksmith is giving a demonstration in about fifteen minutes, and after that we could check out the woodworkers. I thought I might be able to find a train or truck for Robbie."

"He'd like that. I'll have to check anything you pick to make sure it doesn't have any small parts that could come off or sharp edges that could hurt him."

"Okay." Natalie couldn't remember Andie being as hovering with the twins as she seemed to be with Robbie, and she'd still been home when the twins were four.

At the jewelers' exhibit, Natalie and Andie ran in to a high school friend of Andie's whom she hadn't seen since the woman had moved to Glens Falls several years ago.

"Go ahead to the blacksmith demonstration without me," Andie said with more animation than Natalie had seen since they'd arrived. "I'd like to stay and catch up with Sarah. You can meet me back here after the demonstration."

So much for sister bonding. The kink in her shoulders she'd thought was from the long drive down melted away as she walked to the back room where the smithy was set up. She stopped short at the doorway. Connor was standing on the other side of the room with Jack Hill, looking like an ad for the L.L. Bean man in his plaid wool shirt, jeans and work boots. He glanced over at her and his lips turned up in the start of a smile that he seemed to catch before it became a full smile. She rubbed the back of her neck. Was he happy to see her or not? She wasn't up to trying to read anyone else's signals today.

"Natalie." Jack waved her over.

She skirted around the people milling in front of the smithy's anvil waiting for the demonstration to begin.

"Mom said you were back," Jack said.

"For a while."

Connor drew his lips into a thin line, and her heart

stuttered. Was he unhappy about her possible job at the station in Chicago, that she might be leaving? More likely, he was concerned she wouldn't hold up her commitment to the pageant. She'd set him straight on that at their next practice. Friends didn't let down friends. She'd learned that lesson the hard way.

Jack opened up his arms for a friendly hug that Natalie couldn't refuse without making a fuss.

"What's going on here?"

Natalie jumped back at the woman's words, her foot landing on the toe of Connor's steel-toed boot. His arms went around her waist to keep her from falling, pulling her back against his solid chest. Her mouth went dry at the contrast between Jack's friendly hug and Connor holding her in his arms.

"Natalie, I'm sorry." Jack's wife touched her arm. "I was teasing."

"Suzi, you startled me." Natalie reluctantly untangled herself from Connor. "Are the three of you here together?" She circled her pointer finger around.

"Yep, and my sister, Brianne."

Suzi and Jack, and Brianne and Connor. Two couples. This was a date. Natalie's cheeks warmed as she edged farther away from Connor and looked for Brianne.

"Did I see Andie over at the jewelry exhibit?" Suzi asked.

Natalie nodded. "She ran into a friend she hasn't seen in a while and told me to come ahead and watch the blacksmith demonstration by myself."

"The same with Brianne," Suzi said, "only for her it was about fifteen friends." She gave Connor an apologetic look.

An arranged date. She was surprised Connor hadn't

said anything about it the other night at her house during her mother's matchmaking fiasco. How did he put up with it? He was far more patient than she was.

"The missing returns." Connor smiled, looking over her head toward the doorway.

Brianne was standing there with a reciprocal smile. Natalie tensed. Maybe this wasn't a fix-up. She should go find Andie. The prospect of being a fifth wheel had dimmed the appeal of the blacksmith demonstration.

Brianne made her way across the room tugging a guy Natalie hadn't noticed before behind her.

"Great," Suzi said, frowning.

The tension in the air thickened as the couple drew closer. Natalie glanced at Connor out of the side of her eye. He was still smiling, maybe even more so, adding to her confusion.

"Look who I ran in to." Brianne introduced the man as a high school friend of hers. "He drove his grandmother and her friend here and was sitting in the other room kind of bored. I told him about the blacksmith demonstration." Still gripping the man's hand, she asked, "You don't mind, Connor, do you?"

"Not at all," Connor said.

Natalie flexed her fingers. If she was reading Connor right, and she was pretty sure she was, his earlier smile had been one of relief.

The demonstration began with Natalie sandwiched comfortably between Suzi and Connor.

"Cool," Connor said as the smith bent the molten iron into shape. "I should sign up for a class."

"And, what, set up your own smithy in the old horse barn behind the parsonage?" she teased.

"It never hurts to keep one's work options open."

Natalie couldn't help thinking Connor's words had a double meaning for her.

His gaze traveled to a parishioner standing on the other side of the room. "Of course, if I weren't pastor of Hazardtown Community Church, I wouldn't have access to the barn."

Natalie stared at the man for a moment. One of his detractors? He lifted a hand in greeting to Connor and her. She waved back. Was that a possibility, the church not renewing Connor's contract? Mom had said not to worry. Natalie furtively searched Connor's profile. His jaw was set. Fixation on the show, or in concern about his pastorate?

"Hey," Connor said when the blacksmith finished, "I'm going to go up and ask a couple of questions. Where can I meet up with you guys after?"

"Furniture," Suzi said, and Jack rolled his eyes. She slugged him in the shoulder. "I just want to look."

"Right." He grinned, and Connor and her sister laughed.

Obviously, some kind of inside joke. Natalie felt herself fading into the background. What had she expected? Connor to leave his friends and his date—arranged or not—to hang out with her and Andie?

"Nice seeing you all," she said. "I'd better go find Andie."

"Natalie." Her sister's friend, Sarah, was rushing across the emptying room. "It's Andie. Something's wrong. She's having chest pains and trouble breathing."

"Where is she? Is someone with her?"

"My sister. She's calling 911."

Connor sensed Natalie's fear even before the bits of the woman's words he overheard registered with him. He turned heel and followed her. He was sure Brianne wouldn't mind him stepping out of the picture. And Jack and Suzi would understand. Considering his and Jack's history, maybe too well. It was his job, but more, it was *Natalie*. She'd need someone with her.

Connor touched Natalie's shoulder. She jerked. "Oh, Connor. It's Andie."

"I heard." He lengthened his stride to keep up with Natalie's run.

"Where is she?" Natalie asked the woman with her when they reached the jewelers' exhibit.

"I don't know. I left her here with my sister."

Natalie's gaze darted around the room as if she might have somehow missed seeing Andie. Connor wrapped his hand around hers and squeezed. She looked up with a trembling smile.

"Are you Natalie?" one of the exhibitors asked.

"Yes," he answered for her.

"They took your sister to an office off the reception area to lie down."

"Thanks," Natalie said, taking off at the same speedy pace.

As soon as they entered the reception area, a woman with an infant rushed from a room behind the counter. "I don't know what happened," the woman babbled. "She was holding Ben, and all of a sudden she fell apart. I thought she was going to drop him."

Natalie pushed by her, yanking her hand from his. "This is my fault," she said, heading to the room the woman had come from.

Connor resisted his initial urge to race after her. "Thanks," he said to the two women. "I'm her pastor. I'll take care of things now."

"I called 911," the woman with the baby said.

"Yes, I know." His voice sounded brusque, but he wanted to be with Nat when she saw Andie.

"If I give you my cell phone number, would you call when you know how Andie is?" her friend asked.

"Of course." He reined in his impatience and plugged the woman's number into his phone.

"Thanks. I'll say a prayer."

Since he didn't remember Andie's friend from school, he didn't know if she was sincere or saying that because he was a pastor. While normally that would have bothered him, at the moment he didn't care. The thought was enough.

When he finally entered the office where Andie had been taken, he found Natalie sitting on the leather couch next to her sister, who was lying back with a cloth on her forehead. He didn't know which of them looked paler. *Andie's the one you need to tend to first*, he reminded himself.

"Connor, I'm glad you were here," Andie said. "I'm scared."

Natalie stood and let him take her place. She walked to the head of the couch.

He took Andie's hand. "The emergency squad will be here soon. What happened?"

"I don't know. I was holding the baby, Ben. He's such a cutie, just like Robbie was. I started crying for no reason."

A motion from Natalie caught his attention. She signed him, *I'll tell you later.*

A moment of melancholy overtook him. They'd each taken a short class in American Sign Language in college and had used it to share silent comments.

Andie sniffed as if she might cry again, bringing him back to the present.

"Then, my heart started pounding and I couldn't catch

my breath. Little Ben's mother grabbed him from me as if I'd drop him. I'd never drop a baby."

"I know you wouldn't," he soothed her.

"I was afraid I was having a heart attack. Remember Mike Fuest? He's only a couple of years older than I am, and he had a heart attack."

"And he's fine now," Connor said of his parishioner. "How do you feel now?"

Andie rubbed the right side of her chest. "It still hurts."

"Would you like me to pray with you?" He motioned Natalie to take her sister's other hand without waiting for Andie's affirmation, and he took hers. "Dear Lord, watch over Your daughter Andrea and, according to Your wishes, make her strong and well. In Your name, amen." *And*, he added silently, *use me as You see fit to give Natalie whatever it is she needs to be whole again*.

"Excuse me." An EMT from the Hadley-Luzerne Emergency Medical Services interrupted the silence following Connor's plea. "Is she the possible heart attack we got the call about?"

A panicked look passed over Andie's face when the EMT said "heart attack." Connor couldn't tell if it was fear of that possibility, or fear the EMT might discover she was faking. God forgive him. That was harsh, but knowing her and Natalie's relationship, he wouldn't put it past Andie not to pull a stunt like this to make Nat feel bad, to get back at her for whatever it was that Andie held against Natalie.

Natalie dropped his hand and placed herself between the man and Andie like a lioness defending its young. "My sister is the person you were called about. She's had some kind of episode."

"Please step aside and let us assess the situation."

Connor rose from the couch and went to Natalie. Placing his arm around her shoulder, he urged her back out of the way so the other emergency personnel could roll a stretcher into the room. Despite her bristle a moment ago, or because of it, Natalie felt as soft and limp as a rag doll. They watched the emergency techs take Andie's vital signs.

"I don't think it's her heart," Natalie said in a low voice the others couldn't hear. "Because it started when she held the baby, I think it was a panic attack, maybe brought on by postpartum depression." In confidence, she shared what her mother had told her about Andie's miscarriage. "I couldn't put my finger on it before today, but to me she's acting like the wife of one of my colleagues at the last station who was diagnosed with postpartum depression."

He felt like a heel for the thoughts he'd had about Andie earlier when he'd doubted her. "Should we say something to the EMT?"

Natalie glanced at her sister, who the EMT had sitting up on the couch. "No, not yet. It could just be me. I think she's been acting odd since I arrived. It may have been gradual, so no one else has noticed. Or maybe I'm imagining things. You know, Andie has always had her 'moods.' If they take her to the hospital because of something I say and it turns out to be nothing, I'll never hear the end of it. Unless she stops me, I'll stay with her when the doctor sees her and say something then if I feel I need to."

"Miss," the EMT said, motioning Natalie over.

"They want to take me to the hospital," Andie said. "But I've got the kids, Rob, work."

"They just want to have a doctor check you over," Natalie assured her.

"What if they want to keep me there?"

Natalie bit her lip.

"You should go with the medics," Connor said, relieving Natalie of having to tell Andie what to do and risking her resistance. "Natalie and I'll follow the ambulance."

"You'll stay?"

"Of course," Natalie said.

"Connor, too?"

"Yes, I'll come with Natalie and stay."

Natalie squeezed Andie's hand, and the emergency technicians wheeled her away.

Connor pulled out his phone. "I'm going to text Jack, and then we can leave." He typed in his message and waited for a reply. "All set."

Natalie gave him a crooked smile. "I really appreciate your help," she said, "and I'm sorry we crashed your date."

"Not a problem." *More of a relief.* "I have a strong feeling Brianne is glad to have me out of the picture."

"With some people, there's no accounting for taste." Natalie covered her mouth with her fingertips. "We'd better get to the hospital. I have Mom's car parked out front."

Connor placed his hand on the small of her back and walked her out of the office. An afternoon at the Glens Falls hospital wasn't exactly his fantasy of spending time with Natalie, but he'd take it.

"I'll drive," Connor said, holding his hand out for the keys.

"I can—" Natalie began, but stopped. "No." She dropped the keys in his hand. She was too rattled by

Andie and by whatever was going on between her and Connor. Ministering to Andie was his job, but she felt— or hoped—his actions meant more.

Connor opened the car door for her before walking around to the driver's side. "Thanks again," she said, "for coming with me, giving up your afternoon."

"No problem." He started the car and headed toward the county highway. "There are times when my work has to come first."

She swallowed her disappointment and chided herself for being so selfish. Of course he was coming with her to the hospital for Andie. He'd probably be a lot more comfort to her sister than she would.

He turned onto the highway. "And as setups go, today doesn't come close to your mother's attempt the other night."

She flushed. "You're saying that because of the cookies." Her flush deepened. Could she have said anything more lame or self-serving?

"That and a comment Josh made about being willing to step in for me today. He said something about keeping his options open that rubbed me the wrong way."

Connor didn't sound like she'd expect Pastor Connor to sound. She stared at the road ahead of them. He and Josh had always had a sibling rivalry, not unlike her and Andie's. She glanced at his profile as he turned into the hospital parking lot. A smile tugged at the corner of his mouth.

"You did that to get my mind off Andie," she said, breaking into a slow smile.

"I'm not telling." He found a parking space near the emergency room and parked.

She stuck her tongue out at him in a childish gesture

she'd often used when he bested her at something. It was fun to just be herself with Connor, with anyone. She'd gotten far too used to playing for the camera.

He met her on her side of the car and they walked to the building. She dragged her feet as they closed in on the emergency room. Connor held the door for her, and despite the brightly painted walls all the lightness drained out of her when she crossed the threshold. People waiting to be seen sat sporadically dispersed in the hard plastic chairs ringing the entry room. A baby cried, and Connor squeezed her shoulder.

She hurried over to the glass-enclosed desk and tapped her foot as she waited for the clerk on the other side to slide open the window. "The Luzerne Emergency Squad bought my sister in. Andie—Andrea Bissette."

"Spell the last name please."

"B-i-s-s-e-t-t-e."

The clerk typed into the computer. "E7. I'll buzz you into the door on your right."

"Thank you." Natalie and Connor walked to the right and when the buzzer sounded, she pulled the doorknob of the heavy metal door. As it cracked open, Connor reached over her, grabbed the door edge and lifted the weight from her as he'd already done several times this afternoon—and countless times in the past.

"Oh," the clerk said when they emerged on the other side. "I didn't know you had someone else with you. We only allow one person per patient. One of you will have to wait outside."

"I'm the patient's pastor," Connor said.

A commotion arose in the entry. The clerk looked through the glass and hit the buzzer. The door next to her and Connor flew open to let in an emergency technician pushing a gurney with an apparent stabbing victim, followed by two police officers escorting another man with lesser wounds.

The clerk frowned. "I guess it's okay since you're here in an official capacity." She waved Natalie and Connor on and trained her attention on the new arrivals.

"Does that work often, using your pastor cred?" Natalie asked.

"Often enough." He pulled at the neck of his long-sleeved T-shirt. "Looks like the Es are to the right."

They walked by the central nursing station to E7.

"About time," Andie said when they walked into her glass-partitioned area.

This was the Andie Natalie was used to. *She must be feeling better.* "We came as quickly as we could."

"Has anyone been in to see you?" Connor asked.

"Only a nurse to take my temperature, pulse and blood pressure." Andie fidgeted with the blanket that had been placed over her. "It's freezing in here."

"Do you want your jacket?" Natalie reached under the gurney where she'd spied it. If anything, the room was too warm.

"Yes, and maybe we should leave."

Natalie held the jacket in her hand, hesitating to hand it to her sister for fear she'd take the action as encouragement to leave.

"Andie." Connor touched her arm as if to restrain her. "You need to stay until a doctor checks you out. You were not okay at the Folk School. What would you do if you were home alone with Robbie and you had a similar episode? I think he'd be frightened."

Andie gripped the blanket with white knuckles. "I'd never do anything to hurt Robbie."

What was Andie's obsession with not hurting kids? Everyone knew Andie adored kids of all ages.

"I didn't hurt the baby," Andie said.

Confusion spread across Connor's face.

"Of course you didn't," Natalie said after a moment of silence.

"Right. I talked with your friend and her sister before we left the festival," Connor said, obviously thinking Andie meant her friend's baby nephew. "Your friend wanted to give me her phone number so I could let her know how you were. The baby was fine. He waved bye-bye to us."

Her heart cracked. Connor's words hadn't wiped any of the pain off her sister's face.

"You're pregnant?" asked the nurse, who'd breezed in time to hear Andie's comment about not hurting the baby. "You didn't say that in the medical history we took when you came in."

Natalie bit her lip. *Andie must feel she did something to cause her miscarriage.*

"No." Andie's voice caught. "I'm not pregnant."

"You need to tell her." Natalie's gaze drilled into Andie's.

"You know?" Andie said in an almost inaudible voice.

Natalie nodded. "Robbie said something to me when I was babysitting him about the Christmas baby not coming and you crying. I asked Mom, and she told me."

"I asked her not to."

Natalie squeezed her sister's coat in her folded arms. This wasn't the time for one of their petty arguments.

Andie tilted her head toward Connor.

"I told Connor," Natalie admitted, answering her sister's silent question.

"Great," Andie said. "Let's make sure the whole world knows my private business."

Natalie tried to ignore the way her sister's words slashed through her. Andie was hurting. But she was Andie's sister, not the whole world.

"Andie, Natalie told me in pastor confidence. Nothing she said or you say will go beyond me."

"All right, then. I had a miscarriage in September." She said it as if she was admitting to a crime.

"I'll need the information," the nurse said. "Would you like them to leave?"

"I'll go," Connor said. "You let me know if you need me today or later."

"Thanks, *Pastor* Connor. I'll do that."

"Promise?" he asked.

"Promise."

Natalie's heart swelled with pride for the professional Connor had become. Not that she'd had any part in it. "I'll go, too," she said, watching Connor leave. "Unless you want me to stay."

"No, you can go," Andie said, dismissing her.

Natalie refused to leave on a bad note. She stashed Andie's coat back under the gurney, leaned over and hugged her sister's stiff form until she relented and hugged her back. "Tell her everything," she said for Andie's hearing only. "It will help the doctor." Natalie felt Andie's nod. She straightened, swallowing to break the block of apprehension in her chest. "I'll call Mom and let her know what's going on."

Connor paced the waiting room off the emergency room entryway. In the background, the all-news channel blared about a fast-moving nor'easter that had veered inland and was heading for Northeastern New York.

"Expect up to three feet or more of snow in the higher elevations," the weathercaster said.

Connor glanced out the window at the fat flakes drifting down in winter splendor, knowing all too well how fast they could change to a blinding veil of windblown white. He sat in a chair facing away from the window. *Andie must have let Natalie stay.* His professional side yearned to counsel them to resolve their differences. His ordinary-man side wanted to align with Natalie and protect her from the hurt Andie was so good at inflicting on her.

He pulled out his cell phone and made use of the hospital's public Wi-Fi to check his email. One from an old friend from seminary caught his attention.

"Hey, am I interrupting?"

Natalie was standing right beside his chair. "You looked so engrossed," she said.

He clicked off his phone. "Checking email. I thought Andie might have let you stay."

She sat next to him. "No. I called Mom and talked with her a while. I think I might have made a connection with Andie."

"Good." He tapped his fingers on the hard plastic armrest of his chair, mulling over what his fellow seminarian had emailed him and whether to share it with Natalie. "Do you want to get coffee or something? We missed lunch."

"I'm not really hungry." She brushed the leg of her jeans. "Would you come with me to the chapel and pray that Andie tells the doctor the full story?" She glanced around the waiting room. "I'd feel more comfortable there. The nurse said it's just up the hall."

"Anything you want."

"You could get yourself in trouble with an offer like that." She stood and grabbed her coat from where she'd dropped it on the seat next to her when she'd come in.

Looking up into her coffee-brown eyes, all he could think was in trouble might be exactly where he wanted to be. He stood and walked with Natalie to the chapel, casually looping his arm around her waist and reveling in the simple joy of Natalie not pulling away.

He lifted his arm to open the chapel door. "Do you want me to pray with you?"

She touched his arm. "Thank you, but not out loud." She slid her hand into his. "What I want to say is too personal."

He slid his fingers into hers, mentally contrasting the size of her hand and the softness of her skin with his. He of anyone should respect her request, and he did. But that didn't stop him from feeling shut out. They walked down the aisle to the front pew and kneeled. Connor glanced at Natalie, her head bowed, eyes closed. What was it about her that ripped open the wounds of his old insecurities? She stirred beside him, and he tore his gaze from her. Closing his eyes, he prayed for Andie and Natalie—and for strength and clarity for himself.

When they finished, Connor talked Natalie into getting something to eat before they returned to the ER waiting room.

"Pretty." Natalie stood by the window. "I love the way fresh snow makes everything look so clean and sparkly."

Connor stood behind her. He'd been thinking the same, but not about the snow.

"Natalie." Andie stood in the doorway.

Natalie brushed by him, breaking the tenuous connection between them, and rushed to her sister.

"I can go home," Andie said, followed by something else in a low voice he couldn't hear.

Natalie nodded. "I'll get my coat."

Connor lifted her jacket from the chair next to him and walked over. He held it for her.

"Thanks." She slipped her arms in and pulled it on. "We better get going before we get snowed in here."

Andie looked past them to the window. "I didn't know it was snowing. Connor, will you drive?"

"I could." He glanced at Natalie. She dropped her gaze to the floor and tapped her foot.

"It's not that you're a bad driver, Natalie. But I'm not used to riding with you," Andie said.

Andie wasn't used to riding with him, either. Connor zipped his coat, waiting for some confirmation from Natalie.

Her foot tapping stopped. "That's a good idea, if Connor doesn't mind."

"It's fine." He certainly wasn't going to tell her that he'd feel better if he was driving, too. But maybe she'd remembered that he wasn't a comfortable passenger. When they'd been together, he'd insisted on driving so often she'd teased him that she had her own personal chauffer.

Natalie handed him the keys, and he walked ahead to open the door for them. When they reached the car, he popped the trunk to get the scraper to clear the snow off the car and let Andie in the backseat. He reached for the front door handle.

"Natalie, sit with me so we can talk," Andie said.

"Okay, but why don't I start the car so it can warm up while Connor cleans the snow off." Natalie pushed the door closed and walked with him around the front of the car. "Do you mind my sitting in the back with Andie? Since she wants me, I'd like to be there for her."

"No, it's fine."

"Thanks." Natalie pulled her wool cap down farther over her ears against the blustering wind and leaned against the car fender.

How could he mind? He knew how much Natalie wanted Andie and her to get along. She always had. Maybe this was the start of their mending. He handed her back the keys to start the car and lifted the windshield wipers so he could brush off the snow.

Natalie tilted her head and smiled at him. "Has anyone told you lately what a nice guy you are?" She ducked in the car before he could answer.

He attacked the thick layer of ice that had formed on the windshield with a vengeance so he had an excuse for the warmth that filled him and didn't have to acknowledge to himself that it had a lot more to do with Natalie's smile and words than the energy he was exerting.

Chapter Eight

Natalie clutched the car's armrest with an iron grip, resting her left arm on her lap to block Connor's view. He wasn't the only one who was more comfortable with him doing the driving today. But as much as she normally liked to be the person behind the wheel, she'd always deferred to Connor. She'd sensed the younger Connor had a need to grab control of whatever he could because so many parts of his life seemed out of anyone's control.

She filled her lungs and breathed out slowly. It was a toss-up what was worse: the view she'd had of Connor's rigid shoulders from the backseat as he'd driven through the storm to Andie and Rob's house, or the full view of the blinding snow she had now from the from the front seat as he maneuvered from her sister's house to the parsonage.

"Thinking about Andie?" Connor asked. "I'll give Rob a call tomorrow. Feel him out about the situation and what he thinks he could do."

"That's a good idea. You know Rob isn't big on talking. But he's had to have noticed Andie isn't herself. It might be a relief for him to have you take the first step."

Connor corrected his steering as the car went into a slight skid. "Sometimes it's part of my job to be interfering."

"Like your parishioners." A smile spread across Natalie's face, as she remembered the twins trapping them in the parsonage attic.

"I tend to be more compassionate and less obvious. Or, at least I try to. They're well-meaning for the most part."

"Slow down." Natalie grabbed his arm and then thought better. He'd need both hands to control the car. "There's a red flasher."

"Yes, Natalie, I see it," he said in controlled syllables. "I'm only going twenty-five."

"Sorry. I'm a little wound-up."

He patted her knee, and she tensed because he'd taken his hand off the wheel. He slowed to a stop at the intersection of the state highway the parsonage was located on. A fire department vehicle, lights flashing, blocked the turn onto that road. A well-bundled figure with a Schroon Lake Volunteer Fire Department reflective vest walked over to Connor's side of the car. Connor rolled the window half-down, and snow blew in hard enough to sting her cheek on the other side of the car.

"Hey, Connor," Josh said over the collar of his coat, which was rolled up to protect his face. He looked across the seat.

Josh was a volunteer firefighter? Natalie resisted the urge to slouch down and pull her scarf up to hide her face. She straightened. Interfering parishioners aside, there was no reason Josh shouldn't see her with Connor.

"Natalie," Josh said.

She fidgeted. She could almost see the slow, inviting smile, which was strikingly similar to his brothers', spreading across Josh's face behind his collar.

Connor waved his hand in front of his brother's face, a muscle working in his jaw.

His territorial attitude made her stomach do a little flip-flop that had nothing to do with the hospital coffee she'd had or her frazzled nerves.

"Ken Healy lost it on the curve and overturned his fuel-oil truck almost in front of the church."

"Anyone hurt?" Connor asked.

"Not badly. No one was coming from the other direction. The emergency squad took Ken up to the hospital in Saranac Lake to be checked out. He said he was fine, got out and was walking around when we got here."

"I'll call the hospital and check on him when I get home."

"You're not getting home anytime soon, unless you're walking. The truck is across both lanes. And, if the truck's leaking oil, we may be evacuating the Hazardtown area anyway." Josh dug in his pocket. "I'll give you the key to my apartment. You can drop Natalie off and stay with me." He pushed his key ring through the window toward Connor. "It's the…" Josh stopped and ran his gaze over the car as if just realizing it wasn't Connor's. "Or maybe you have a better offer?"

Connor pursed his lips.

Was he annoyed by Josh's offer or his comment?

"Mom and Dad's house is closer," Natalie said. "I'm sure they wouldn't mind putting you up for a night. There's no sense in doing any extra driving." No matter how awkward his staying might be after her mother's fix-up attempt the other night, she owed him. Connor had certainly run interference for her with her family enough times lately.

"Yeah, sure. That's a better idea." Josh closed his fist around his keys and shoved them back in his coat pocket. "You don't want to be driving back to your folks' from my place in this." Josh gestured at the snow.

"Keep warm," Natalie said as Connor rolled the window up.

"Thanks," Connor said. "Your parents won't mind me staying?" He turned the car around and headed back in the other direction.

"My parents? Do you even have to ask?"

"True. This is different, but I'll never be able to thank them enough for all the times in high school they gave me someplace to go to when my dad was on a drunken rampage and Mom was working nights."

She touched his arm, filled with compassion for Connor. As an adult, she could see Connor's home situation a lot clearer than she did as a teen.

"As much as Josh has been irritating me lately, he did protect me from Dad as best he could." He cleared his throat. "Then he got called up with his National Guard unit to go to Afghanistan and was wounded."

"Yeah, I was afraid you were going to give up your scholarship to Houghton because you didn't want to leave your mom alone. Just when we had everything planned out the way I wanted it. Pretty selfish of me."

He placed his hand over hers. "I can see now that it was better for Mom to leave and go live with my aunt."

"Things look different at twenty-seven than they do at seventeen," Natalie said, thinking as much about Connor and her as she was about Connor and his family.

He stared straight ahead. "Once Josh got home from

the army hospital, we never got back the closeness we had as kids."

Natalie slumped in the seat, struggling to breathe past the weight on her chest. She'd done the same thing to her family and more so to Connor. Pushed them away. It wasn't that her family was making her an outsider. She was the one who'd gone away and cut the ties. The call from her agent replayed in her mind. And she was poised to do it again.

The car skidded into the oncoming lane, and she bumped up against the hard wall of Connor's shoulder. In one fluid motion, he brought the car back into their lane.

Strong, solid, dependable Connor. He was always there for her. Her heart ached. As much as she yearned to rebuild what they'd had and more, she couldn't see any way to do it.

Connor sat alone on the couch in the room off the Delacroix's TV room. After Natalie's mother had welcomed him with open arms for the night, she'd sat Natalie and him down at the table for the remainder of the boisterous family dinner. Afterward, he'd needed a break from the constant conversation. He'd grown too used to living alone. When Natalie and her siblings declined his offer to help them with the dishes and her parents moved to the living room to watch the news, he wandered out to the front room off the living room.

Like the rest of the house and its residents, this room hadn't changed much since he'd last been in it. Originally the house's formal parlor, it still had its high ceiling and exposed beams, making it a perfect spot for the family's Christmas tree. He sank into the soft cushions of the overstuffed couch and let the blinking lights of the tree and the blazing fire in the woodstove lull him almost to sleep.

"Mom said I'd find you here."

He blinked wide awake as Natalie walked to the couch and sat next to him.

"It's so peaceful in here," she said. "I see why Mom has always come in here to read, rather than staying in the living room with everyone else. The quiet and privacy."

She leaned her head back on the cushion behind her, and he flirted with the idea of letting his arm drop from the back of the couch to her shoulder. It seemed so natural.

"There's always someone around," she said.

He whipped his gaze to the doorway and like a teen caught kissing on the front porch, he backed off by casually stretching and resting his arm back on the couch behind Natalie.

"I miss the solitude of my own place."

"I was thinking almost the same thing before you came in, that I've gotten used to having my evenings to myself."

"Want me to leave?" she asked, straightening.

"No," he said quickly. "I'm not sure being alone so much is a good thing."

"Nor something the church ladies are likely to encourage."

He laughed, throwing off the momentary feeling of abandonment that the thought of Natalie leaving had stirred in him. "You don't think this is another setup, do you, leaving us in here alone?"

"Even if it is, I say let's enjoy it while we can. Claire

and Paul were talking about getting a game of Dominion going."

Connor inched his arm back toward her shoulder. He was enjoying it already. The warm glow of the fire, the twinkling of the tree lights and Natalie's nearness wrapping him in a blanket of belonging. His cell phone chimed, making them both start. He shifted to grab it out of his pocket, and Natalie moved away as if she had realized just how close they were sitting.

He frowned as he read the text from Josh. You're doing me proud, baby bro. When you said double date, I didn't know you meant two dates with different women. He clicked off the screen.

"Bad news?" Natalie asked. "Or something you can't talk about?"

"It was Josh."

"About the accident?"

"No, Josh being Josh."

"Ah, enough said."

Connor settled back on the couch, appreciative of Natalie's understanding without him having to say any more. His hip caught the corner of the other overstuffed couch cushion, tilting Natalie his way. As if beyond his control, he slipped his arm down the back cushion until it rested around her shoulder. A sense of well-being filled him as they sat in silence looking at the Christmas tree. He could sit like this forever.

"Your tree at the parsonage must be pretty, too."

"I guess." He didn't tell her he hadn't turned the lights on or even looked at it.

She folded her hands in her lap and rubbed her thumbs together. "Did Hope insist on putting the star on top? I'm sorry about that."

"No. What did Hope have to do with the Christmas star?"

Natalie stared at her thumbs. "The star was in the box she brought down from the attic with you. She wanted to put it on the tree, and I tried to discourage her by saying it was old and that you and she could go shopping for a new one. That's what upset her last Sunday afternoon."

"Then you didn't throw it in my trash in the garage."

She lifted her head, looked at him. "I couldn't throw it out. I packed it away." She paused as if waiting for a reaction from him.

He set his jaw so she wouldn't see him struggle to control his emotions. "How did it get here?"

Her gaze flitted away and back. "Like I said, I couldn't throw it away. I found it when I was cleaning out my apartment in Syracuse to move to Chicago. I brought it back to Mom and Dad's with my other college stuff before I left. Later, I told Mom to give anything of value in those boxes to someone who could use them and to throw the rest out."

She couldn't throw it away, but she could give it away. He didn't know what he'd expected her to say or why her explanation bothered him so much.

"Mom gave it to the Bargain Shed. I can only guess that the former pastor or his wife must have picked it up."

"Could be. Jared and Becca didn't use it last year. They must not have seen it in the attic. It was kind of hidden among some other boxes." Connor spent a moment mulling whether finding the star was God directing him or his own wishful thinking. "What did Hope say?"

Natalie sank back into the cushion, and he tightened his embrace. "She said the star was beautiful like the one she and her grandmother had and that you were going to love it. Her words broke my heart, but I couldn't let the church women put the star on the tree. Not without letting you know first."

His insides melted. Natalie had guessed his feelings about the star, even though he hadn't said anything about them. "It's getting better, but we never know what might set Hope off."

Natalie leaned her head on his shoulder. "I am sorry. Do you think she put the star in the trash?"

"I do now," he said into her hair, breathing in its lightly floral scent. "I'll talk with her."

"Tell her I'm sorry I upset her."

"I will." He closed his eyes and absorbed their momentary closeness.

"Here you are." Claire burst in the room. "We've decided to watch the country-music Christmas special. Want to join us?"

Connor lifted his head and immediately missed the warmth of the contact with Natalie. "Maybe in a minute. I want to get Natalie's take on something I'm thinking about doing."

Claire lifted an eyebrow and grinned. She was as bad as Josh.

"Like Connor said, we'll be in in a minute." Natalie's irritation was evident to him, if not to her sister, who took her time sauntering out.

Once Claire had left, Natalie looked up at him expectantly.

He folded and unfolded his arms. "Have you heard back from your agent about the job in Chicago?"

"No, he said the station would call me directly. Why?"

Connor rubbed his palms down the front of his jeans. "I kind of have a job offer in suburban Chicago."

Her eyes lit, sparking his heart. Then they dimmed, extinguishing the flame before it could flare. He plunged ahead, uncertain about what her reaction meant. "A friend of mine from seminary has a church there. He was a couple years ahead of me and kind of a mentor." Connor bit the side of his mouth to stop rambling. He was making a bigger deal out of this than it was. "He's looking for an assistant pastor, primarily a youth pastor. At school, I wrote a paper outlining a program idea I have for ministering to older youth and young adults to get them more active in their local churches. A lot of college students seem to take a hiatus from church participation until they marry and have kids old enough for Sunday school." He was rambling again.

"True. I did for a while," she admitted. "You'd be good. But aren't you happy at Hazardtown Community? It was your dream, at least at one time."

He analyzed her words, working the muscle in his jaw. She had a job possibility in Chicago but wanted him to stay in Paradox Lake? It sounded like she didn't want him in her life outside Paradox Lake any more than she had before. His heart crashed.

"Being the pastor of Hazardtown Community was— still is—my dream job. But my contract is up in January, and I know there are still people in the congregation, on the administrative council, who don't think Jerry Donnelly's son can be an effective pastor here. As Josh says, I need to keep my options open." *Maybe in more ways than one.* He avoided her gaze, fearing he'd see agreement on her face.

"Claire is on the council, and Mom said she saw no problem renewing your contract. Everyone loves you," she blurted. A pink tinge spread across her cheekbones.

He tried to ignore the heat radiating through his chest. *She isn't talking about herself.* "My friend texted me. I plan to call him back for details."

She nodded against his shoulder. He reached and lifted her chin until she faced him, planning to reassure her that she didn't have to be embarrassed. As much as he wished otherwise, he knew what she meant.

Her eyes widened, pupils dilated. All of his feelings for Natalie, old and new, welled in him. He had no choice. He lowered his head and pressed his lips to hers, letting his emotions overtake his reasoning. Pulling her closer, all he could think was that she tasted warm and sweet, and despite anything she might say to the contrary, was as much his as she'd ever been.

Natalie awoke for the umpteenth time, not able to get the memory of Connor's kiss out of her mind. Everything that had seemed so right last night—the closeness of sitting in the front room looking at the Christmas tree, their kiss, watching the Christmas music special together with Mom and Dad and her siblings as if he was a part of the family—seemed all wrong this morning. She pulled the covers over her head at the thought of seeing Connor at breakfast. How was she going to face him today, knowing that she couldn't be what he'd always wanted her to be? The pastor's wife. Not here, where there were no avenues for her to pursue her career. Not in the Chicago area, where her reputation could be as much an albatross to him as his father's reputation was in Paradox Lake.

She rolled off her bed and kneeled beside it. *Dear Lord, thank You for last night and for clearing my eyes of the mists of what could have been. I've always known that Connor has great works he needs to do for You, whether they're here or elsewhere. Please don't let me selfishly get in the way. I can't let him give up what he has here for the church in Chicago if it's only because of me.* She bit her lip. *I know I'm not deserving of him or of Your forgiveness for my transgressions, which You have so lovingly given me. Nor should I always be on the asking side when talking to You. But please help me keep my relationship with Connor as strictly that of a good friend no matter how much I may want it, or Connor may think he wants it, to be otherwise. In Your name, Amen.*

There was a knock on her door, followed by her sister saying, "Hey, sleepyhead. You'd better get up or you're going to miss service." The directive brought Natalie to her feet.

"I'm up," she said. "I'll be right down." Natalie dressed for church and went downstairs to join her family.

"Want me to put on a couple more pancakes?" Claire asked as she entered the kitchen. "Paul ate all the ones I cooked."

He grinned at her as he stuffed the last bite in his face and left.

"No, thanks." She walked to the coffeemaker. "Toast and coffee is fine." She glanced at the table. "Where are Mom and Dad?" And Connor?

"They left a couple of minutes ago to drive Connor to the parsonage. Josh texted him last night that they got the fuel-oil truck righted and towed away without any spill, so the fire department didn't have to evacuate the area."

Emptiness drilled through her. Of course, Connor had to go home and get ready for service. She had to get ahold of herself. Five minutes ago, she'd dreaded seeing him. Now she was disappointed because she wouldn't. "Mom and Dad are going right over to church then?" She poured her coffee and popped a couple of slices of whole wheat bread in the toaster.

Claire started the water for dishes. "Yes, I think Mom wanted to walk down the aisle to the organ before the church is too filled. It's her first Sunday back and I think she's self-conscious about using the walker."

"That would be Mom," Natalie said, buttering her toast and carrying her breakfast to the table.

Her sister turned off the water and warmed her cup of coffee before sitting down across from Natalie. "I'm almost glad Andie had that episode yesterday. I've been worried about her since she lost the baby."

"I wondered if anyone else thought she was acting unlike herself or if it seemed that way to me because I don't see her all of the time like you do."

"I mentioned it to Mom, but she said Andie would snap out of it soon. You know how Mom can be sometimes. We're all strong. We can handle our problems ourselves."

Natalie took a bite of toast. *If only saying that made it true.*

"Well, I'm glad Andie got some help. I'm praying she follows up and sees Dr. Hanlon," Claire said.

"Me, too. I think she will. Connor said he'd try to talk with Rob today."

Claire clasped her hands, pointer fingers up, and aimed them at Natalie. "Speaking of Connor, you two looked pretty cozy last night."

The bite of toast dried in her mouth, making it almost impossible to swallow.

"Ah, speechless. Does that mean that you two have resolved whatever came between you at college?"

No, and now if she didn't do something fast, both she and Connor might be running into potential disaster. Natalie made a split-second decision to confide in Claire—up to a point. "Last night was a mistake. We got caught up in nostalgia and the season. Or at least I did."

"Are you sure? You two had something everyone thought was good and solid. We all expected him to propose that Christmas you broke up."

Mom was the only person she'd told about Connor's proposal. "He did."

"What?" Claire placed her coffee mug on the table with a clunk.

"I turned him down for the job in Chicago. I thought it was temporary, that we'd work things out eventually. But it got messy and we went our separate directions."

"You broke up about work?" Claire's tone was incredulous. "I love my work at the research farm, but if I met the right man I could make adjustments."

"And if that right man was a dairy farmer?" Natalie deflected her sister's comment by hitting on Claire's long-standing contention that she wouldn't allow herself to fall in love with a dairy farmer like their dad. She thought it was too hard of a life.

"We're not talking about me," Claire said. "This could be your and Connor's chance to clean up the mess and have a second chance."

Natalie moved a crumb of toast on the table with her finger. "Connor has a job offer in the Chicago area."

"Really? I had no idea he was looking."

"He isn't. It's from a seminary friend. And my agent called me about a possible new job there, too."

"Perfect," Claire said.

"No." Natalie picked up the crumb and dropped it on her plate. "Things aren't the same for me, me and Connor, as they were before." In her heart they weren't. Her feelings for him were even stronger now, but she didn't need to tell Claire that. "Being pastor of Hazardtown Community was, and I think still is, Connor's dream job. He never thought he'd achieve it so quickly after seminary. I'm the person who turned down his marriage proposal for the job I wanted. I couldn't ask him to give up his dream job for me. Even if I did have strong feeling for him, which I'm not saying I do," she quickly added.

Claire quirked one side of her mouth up and knitted her brows.

"I can't say I won't take the job in Chicago again if it's offered to me." Natalie ignored the heavy shadow of foreboding that cloaked her. "Connor's job here isn't really in danger, is it? The council will renew his contract, right?" Natalie hoped that Claire didn't read the rise in her tone as her wanting his contract to be in danger. She didn't want that, even if it would take care of her concerns about Connor choosing to accept the assistant pastor position in Chicago to be near her even if staying here in Paradox Lake was his real calling. That could only lead to him resenting her later.

"Not that I can see," Claire said. "I've even been hearing less grumbling from Connor's die-hard opposition on the council."

"Good." Natalie wished she felt as enthused about that as her answer sounded.

"But…"

Natalie froze for a moment at the force of her sister's voice.

"You do know that if Connor believes Hazardtown Community is where God wants him to be, he wouldn't give up his place here for anyone or anything."

"Autumn said something similar to me. That's good to know. I wouldn't want to come between Connor and his Lord."

"Your Lord, too," Claire gently reminded her. "Have you asked Him what to do?"

"Of course," she insisted and got a skeptical look from Claire.

Natalie stood and picked up her plate to put it in the sink. "I've got to finish getting ready so we won't be late for service. Be back down in five." That would give her time to do her makeup and hair. And it would give her a moment to ask God to forgive her for misleading Claire about her true feelings for Connor. But regardless of her feelings, it was best if she and Connor went their separate ways again after the pageant. Wasn't it? Any feelings Connor might think he had for her were for the girl she'd been, and he'd find out soon enough if he came with her to Chicago that she wasn't that girl anymore. She wouldn't make a mess of his life as she had with her own. All she had to do was keep her feelings hidden for a couple more weeks.

Chapter Nine

"When you see Connor tonight, be sure to tell him again how much I liked his sermon on Sunday." Natalie's mother sat at the kitchen table keeping her company as she finished putting the Tuesday supper plates in the dishwasher.

Natalie closed the dishwasher door, dried her hands and folded the dish towel on the counter before pressing the start button. She listened to it whir to life. Connor had preached about rejoicing in the moments of joy in life and called on all of them to take time this week to discover and celebrate those times. He'd urged them to write down one time during each day that they felt God with them, saying that true joy comes from a security with God—a security that was evident in his passion for the subject and the very way he held himself out to others. Natalie had been hard-pressed to catch even a thread of that security in herself or her life. She'd tried to find times yesterday that she'd felt God with her and had failed. One more thing she and Connor didn't have in common, more ammunition she could use against the pull he exerted on her.

She turned from the counter. "All done." She held her hand out to help her mother from the chair.

Her mother hesitated before taking it. "I'm getting tired of being dependent on everyone."

"Try not to let it bother you. You're doing really well and it's only for a short time." Her throat clogged. *Like the time I have left with you all and Connor.*

Her mother took her hand and pressed her other palm on to the table for support as she rose to her feet. "I talked with Andie today. She said to let you know she's not coming to practice."

Natalie handed her mother her cane. "Is she okay?"

"I think so. Just tired. She said she and Rob got tickets to take Robbie on the Polar Express train ride next Saturday. They wouldn't have spent the money if she didn't feel up to it. Remember the year we took all of you? Renee and Paul couldn't have been more than three."

"Yes. I was in kindergarten. I couldn't wait to talk about it at show-and-tell. It didn't matter that two other kids before me told the same story."

"All of you kids loved Christmas, but I think you loved it most."

Natalie winced. She had until her Christmas breakup with Connor. After that, all of the light had gone out of the season—literally, when she'd taken down her tree and packed the ornaments, including the star, away for good. She'd attended Advent and Christmas services and dutifully sent off gifts to her parents, siblings, nieces and nephew. But she hadn't put up a tree again. Nor had she embraced the joy of the season, of celebrating Christ's birth and the light He brought the world. Talking and being with Connor Saturday night had broken through some of her Christmas darkness, as had his sermon, despite her having trouble applying his words to herself.

"I did—do—love Christmas. Being here with you and Dad and everyone this year is bringing that love back."

"I'm glad for that and for you coming to help me and for what you did for Andie. We were too close to her. We didn't see it coming."

"What I did wasn't that big a deal."

"No, what you did was something big, maybe life-changing. After work today, she stopped in at the community college and picked up some information about their degree in early childhood education. She used to talk about going to college when the kids were all in school. Then, somewhere along the way, she stopped talking about it. Robbie will be in kindergarten in the fall."

Natalie nodded. Her mother's words warmed her, but she couldn't take full credit. She'd drawn her strength to help Andie from Connor. "Connor being there, too, helped a lot."

"I'm sure it was a blessing having him there for you…" Her mother's voice trailed off.

Natalie silently added the missing words *like he used to be.* And, as she'd once thought he'd always be.

"I hope Andie seriously considers taking classes. Working with kids at the church day-care center or as an aide at the elementary school would fit Andie a lot better than her job at the sporting goods store." She hated to admit it, but she was a little jealous of Andie, that she had been able to follow her love for Rob without feeling constrained by a career. Andie was only thirty-two. She could easily pursue a teaching career now, with Rob's support, Natalie was sure. Even Claire, with her soon-to-be-finished advanced degree and job that she loved, sounded like she'd be able to compromise, balance her personal life and work if the right man came along. What was wrong with her? Why did her life seem like an all-or-nothing choice? Or was this God's way of telling her Connor wasn't the man for her?

"Have you heard any more about the job you got the call about last week?" her mother asked.

Natalie shook her head, as much to clear her thoughts as in answer to her mother's question. "My guess is that my agent found out about it too late and the audition slots were already filled." The acknowledgment that she didn't have any job to go back to after Mom recovered opened a void in her—a void she wasn't sure even a callback from her agent could fill.

He mother squeezed her hand. "You can stay here as long as you like. Maybe you should check in with some of the TV stations in Albany after the first of the year. I know it's your life, but I'd like it if you were closer."

"That's an idea," she said, half to humor her mother and half because she wouldn't mind being closer to her family. *Or to Connor*, a voice in her head said. If she lived closer and neither of them had to choose between their work and a relationship... She stopped her thoughts with a frown.

"Maybe not a good idea?" her mother asked.

Natalie wasn't sure what her mother was getting at.

"Your frown," she prompted.

"Sorry. I was thinking about something else. I'll have my agent put out some feelers in Albany."

She helped her mother sit on the living room couch next to her dad, who draped his arm around her, reminding Natalie of her and Connor the other night.

Stepping away, she opened the closet and took out her coat. "I'd better get to practice." She pulled on her coat, said, "Goodbye" and walked out into the wintry night. Maybe the cold air would clear her muddled mind. If she and Connor had any possibility of a real relationship, she wouldn't be considering how the relationship affected her career. Would she? Her mind filled with more questions she couldn't answer. Was that her excuse for not giving in to her true feelings? Was she purposely not listening to what God was telling her because she wanted to hear something different? Or was she just plain overthinking things? Her emotions were too raw and jumbled to know.

As she drove to Sonrise, she prayed for direction for her and Connor. The last thing she wanted to do was to mislead him again.

Connor turned off the light to his church office and closed and locked the door, working hard to throw off the rub of irritation he felt. He should have been at pageant practice forty-five minutes ago. As he'd been getting ready to leave, one of his parishioners had showed up with a "crisis." The crisis being he was lonely. The man was a recovering alcoholic whose wife had left him earlier in the year before he'd gone into recovery and whose children were reluctant to accept that he'd changed. He was afraid he'd be alone for the holidays.

Connor ran his hand over his hair before he yanked on his ski cap. He usually was patient with the man, and he'd tried to reassure him that he had his Savior and his church family at Hazardtown Community. He'd invited the man to the open house at the parsonage next Sunday. But despite his training and best intentions, as the man droned on, Connor couldn't keep his personal thoughts out of his head. The man had brought his loneliness on himself. He could sympathize with the man's children. He'd have a hard time accepting his father, if he was still alive, as sober. Thoughts of his mother and father reminded Connor that sometimes people who thought they were in love just weren't really suited for each other. As much as he believed in the sanctity of the marriage vow, he wouldn't wish his father back into his mother's life.

After the man left, Connor prayed for forgiveness for focusing on himself and becoming impatient with him. Rather than the peace he'd expected his prayer to bring, a chill ran through Connor that had nothing to do with his frigid car. But he and Natalie *were* right for each other, he argued with himself. They always had been and could have been together the past few years if they hadn't both acted like pigheaded children back in college. Saturday had proven that to him, proven it so much that he'd emailed his seminary friend Sunday afternoon to say he might be interested in the assistant pastor position. He and Natalie had their differences, but he was confident they could work them out.

More than an hour later than he'd intended, Connor pulled open the door to the Sonrise Conference Center. He whistled to the strains filtering from the auditorium. They stopped as he stepped in.

"Connor," Jared called from up front near the piano. "We just finished. We'd given up on you."

Jared's cheerful dismissal rubbed him the wrong way as much as his parishioner who'd needed him too much. Connor gauged his stride so he didn't appear to be rushing down to take over from Jared, which is exactly what he felt like doing. He smiled hello to Natalie before facing the choir.

"Sorry, I was delayed. Remember, next Tuesday is dress rehearsal with Becca and the Sunday school kids."

"Covered that," Jared said.

Connor went on anyway. "We'll be meeting an hour earlier, at six, so we won't keep the kids out too late."

"That, too." Jared folded his arms across his chest.

Natalie released a noise that sounded like a cross between a giggle and a choke.

He and Jared *were* acting on the juvenile side, Connor conceded. He'd be the bigger man. He should be thankful his brother had given Natalie a hand. "And I suppose you all know that, if you can't make the earlier time, let me know and come when you can."

"I hadn't gotten to that." Jared grinned.

"We'll see everyone next Tuesday at six, then."

The choir members filed down from the stage risers, with several people stopping to tell Connor they'd be late for the next practice. He assured them it wasn't a problem. He understood work and family commitments came first.

Out of the corner of his eye, he saw Natalie gather her music and push back the piano bench.

"If you can stay a few minutes, we should run through our solo once. This coming week is full and we may not get a chance to before dress rehearsal."

"Covered you there, too," Jared said. "And we sounded good together. Maybe I should have taken the part."

He'd been so focused on Natalie and getting her to stay he hadn't realized Jared was still there. "Don't you need to be getting home?"

"I'm waiting for Josh. He's finishing up the sets."

Wait somewhere else. He glared at Jared.

"Lighten up, bro," Jared said. "I was just busting on you."

"Right." He attempted a conciliatory smile. "The counseling session that delayed me was a tough one." It was easier to blame his tension on his parishioner than to admit, even to himself, that Natalie had him so tied up he was jealous of his brother, his very married brother, spending Connor's time with her.

"You have keys to lock up, so you two can stay and *sing* to your heart's delight."

Connor laughed, letting off more tension. The way Jared had wiggled his eyebrow was as corny as his words.

"Later," Jared said before strolling up the aisle to the door.

"Brothers," Natalie said.

"That's right. You have a couple of them, too." He leaned against the piano.

She adjusted the piano bench and reopened the sheet music. "Ready?" Her smile hit him in the solar plexus like a hard right. He was ready, all right. Ready to share a whole lot more with her than a song. All he needed was to determine if she was, too, before he made a fool of himself again.

Connor's voice blending with hers filled the void inside her like water quenching a powerful thirst. She started her last solo verse with a slight quaver in her voice that made Connor cock his head. She rechanneled the emotion welling in her into the song.

He whistled a cheer when she finished, the sound sending a jolt through her. What she was feeling at the moment went far beyond the friendship she was determined to limit their relationship to.

"You are good," he said.

"You aren't bad yourself." She fumbled with the music, knowing her comment went far beyond his singing.

"Better than Jared?"

She slapped his arm with the folded music. "You're incorrigible."

"I'm not sure that's a quality a pastor should aspire to, but from you, I'll take it as a compliment."

His eyes softened as he offered her his hand. He closed it possessively around hers and pulled her gently to her feet. He was going to kiss her again, and she was powerless to stop him, despite her determination to discourage anything beyond friendship between them. Connor placed his hands on her hips, lowered his head and pressed his lips to hers. As if of their own accord, her arms wrapped around his neck and she kissed him in a way that was anything but friendlike. Connor pulled her closer and the word *lifeline* blared in her head. She should stop him, but she couldn't pull away.

"Natalie, I…" he murmured against her lips.

She pulled back and touched her finger to his lips to stop him from finishing. "We need to talk." The sense of loss that followed was overwhelming. Why couldn't she just accept what Connor's kiss was offering her?

"We do." His voice was husky.

He dropped his hands from around her waist, and she shivered as much from knowing what she had to say probably wasn't what he wanted to hear as from the loss of his closeness.

Connor helped her with her coat, then adjusted her scarf after she'd buttoned up. "Don't you have a hat?"

"No." She stood looking up into his face, relishing his tender touch and concern. Tenderness and concern she didn't deserve, but was all too willing to accept.

In one fluid movement, he pulled his ski cap from his pocket and placed it on her head, yanking it down to cover her ears.

"My hair," she squawked.

"Is beautiful." He wound a strand around his finger, sending a tremor down her spine when his finger caressed her cheek. "Do you want to stop by the parsonage on your way home? To talk. I could brew us up some coffee or hot chocolate."

Her and Connor alone at his house? She fingered the button on her coat. The alternative was her parents' house, and she didn't need to feed their penchant for matchmaking. Maybe they could drive to the diner in Schroon Lake.

"I'll behave myself."

Did he think he was that irresistible? "It's not that."

Connor grinned.

Well, maybe he was that irresistible. "I…" She fumbled for words, glad for the interrupting buzz of his cell phone.

"Excuse me." Connor glanced at the screen, his grin fading. He continued reading and texted back before he clicked the phone off and put it in his pocket.

"Is something wrong?"

"That was Gram. She and Harry are at the parsonage. Their furnace isn't working, so they don't have any heat at their house. Harry wanted to wait it out until someone from the burner service could get out to look at it. Gram insisted on coming over to my house. Harry is just getting over a bout with pneumonia, and I have plenty of room for them to stay."

Connor's step-grandfather, Harry, was well into his eighties. "I wondered why I didn't see him and your grandmother at church service. If you're concerned about my exposing Harry to something, we could go to the diner or my parents' house—or talk another time." She held her breath. The sooner she said what she needed to say, the better.

"It's not that." He shuffled his feet like her little nephew, Robbie, did when he was being shy. "I was hoping for a little privacy."

She slipped her arm in his. "At your house, it's even odds. If we go over to mine, it's four against two."

"I hadn't looked at it that way." He walked her to her car. "I'll follow you up to the house," he said as he closed the car door after her.

Natalie used the five-minute drive from Sonrise to the parsonage to distance herself from the emotions she'd been overwhelmed by the moment before Connor's grandmother had interrupted them. Her relief at knowing she and Connor wouldn't be alone at his house was palpable. Natalie simply couldn't bypass her emotions and think straight when he was near, and she knew only too well the consequences of acting on pure emotion, rather than rational thought. It was a mistake she wasn't going to make again for her sake *and* Connor's.

She let Connor pull into the driveway ahead of her so she'd be able to back out when she left. He parked in the garage and waited in the doorway for her to get out of her car. "I usually go in this way," he said, waving her in before closing the door and leading her through the garage and up the stairs to the kitchen.

An aroma of chocolate and cinnamon tickled Natalie's nose as she stepped in the room, taking her back to times Connor had driven her home from high school by way of his grandmother's. She'd always had a homemade snack for them and some little job she needed Connor to do. That was when his grandmother was a widow and didn't have Harry to do things for her. But Natalie had always thought the jobs were his grandmother's way of boosting Connor's confidence in the shadow of his two older brothers.

"Natalie, it's so good to see you," Connor's grandmother said. "I have hot chocolate all made, and I'm warming up some sugar cookies in the oven."

"It's good to see you, too, Mrs. Stowe." Natalie slipped out of her coat, and Connor hung it on a hook by the outside door.

"Edna, please. We're all adults."

"Edna, then." Natalie watched as Connor strode across the room and snatched a cookie from the pan his grandmother was taking out of the oven.

"Or—" Edna slapped Connor's hand "—most of us are adults. Do you want to have your talk and snack here or in the living room?"

"Here," Natalie said, before Connor could have a chance to say otherwise. In the kitchen, they'd have the table between them.

"Okay." Edna poured two mugs of hot chocolate and placed them on the table with a plate of warm cookies. "Harry and I will be in the other room reading if you need anything else."

Connor leaned over and kissed his grandmother's cheek. "Thanks. We're fine."

Natalie slipped into one of the chairs at the table, hoping Connor would still think they were fine after she'd had her say. She prayed so.

"When we were texting, I told Gram you and I needed to talk about the pageant." He sat in the chair across from her.

"Didn't want to give her the wrong idea?" Natalie teased, thinking about her matchmaking family members.

"The pageant is one of the things I want to cover." He offered her the cookie plate. "These are really good."

She took one. "As good as Autumn's grandmother's snickerdoodles?"

Connor made a show of glancing furtively at the doorway. "I wouldn't want Gram to hear, but no other cookie is as good as Mrs. Hazard's snickerdoodles. But I didn't bring you home to talk about cookies."

Natalie's heart did a little flip-flop at the words *bring you home.*

"I talked with my friend from seminary about his offer." Connor paused, staring into her eyes with an intensity that made her want to look away. "I said I was interested."

She crushed the sweet cookie between her teeth and swallowed. "Are you sure? I talked with Claire on Sunday. She's positive the Hazardtown Community Church administrative council will renew your contract." Her heart raced. She had to get out what she'd come to say. "Please don't rearrange your life for me."

He studied her for what seemed like an eternity.

What if she was wrong about his feelings for her?

She squirmed in the hard wooden chair. But his kisses. Connor wouldn't mislead her. Her conscience pricked her. *Like you misled him back in college?* No, Connor wasn't vindictive. He was a man of God. His eyes shone with an intensity that took her breath away. But he was still a man.

"Because you wouldn't for me?" he finally asked.

Natalie didn't know if he meant past or present.

Connor reached across the table and covered her hand with his. "You know I care for you. I always have."

Care, not love. She sucked in a hard breath. "And I care for you."

His gentle expression melted her to her core. "I won't make a decision without a lot of thought and prayer. And when I do, it won't be because of anything in the past. It'll be because I feel in my heart it's what God wants for me, for us. And I'll accept His answer."

Despite all I've done, he thinks there's an us. Natalie pressed the soles of her feet to the floor to control the joy that rippled through her. "Of course," she agreed once she'd found her voice.

He rubbed her hand with his thumb. "You'll pray, too?"

"I'll pray as hard as I can," she said softly. *Pray not to do anything to hurt you, even if it means I can't be with you.*

Chapter Ten

Connor and Hope sang "Away in the Manger" Saturday evening as they walked the short distance from the parsonage to the church.

"Good thing I brought my flashlight," Hope said, swinging the ray of light in front of them in the dark night. "It used to be Brendon's, but he got a new camping lantern for his birthday."

Connor smiled to himself. He probably could have walked all the way with his eyes closed. "Yes, I'm glad you brought it. The batteries in mine are dead."

"You'd better get some more." She flashed the light around at the trees. "It's dark here, and a little scary. But don't tell Brendon and Ari that. They already think I'm a baby because I like to have a night-light in the bedroom."

"I'd never." He hugged the little girl to his side, pricked by envy of his oldest brother and the family he had with Becca. He glanced down at Hope, with her dark hair and a more delicate version of his father's features. If he and Natalie had a daughter, she might look like Hope. He kicked the snow with his boot. What was he thinking? He didn't know where he and Natalie stood. His grandmother had come back in the kitchen the other night shortly after he'd told Natalie he cared for her. Natalie had used the interruption as an excuse to escape. That's the only way to describe her hasty departure. But she had said she cared for him. Only "caring" could mean anything. He cared for a lot of people but didn't love them, not the way he loved Natalie. He should have laid it out and said he loved her. Then she could have accepted or rejected him and he'd know. Even her saying that she didn't care for him the same way he cared for her would be better than the limbo he was in.

Hope pulled on his jacket. "Connor, you're not paying attention."

"What? I'm sorry."

"I still think you should have worn your pajamas, like me. I read on the Polar Express website that everyone is supposed to."

"But I did. I have on my thermal shirt and long johns. I just wore my jeans over them."

She shook her head. "I don't know. I'll have to see what the other grown-ups have on. You know, I've learned that sometimes you have do things you don't want to get along with others."

Connor bit his lip so as not to chuckle at his little sister's sage advice and then sobered, thinking of his decision to consider his friend's job offer in Chicago. Had he made the decision because he was interested, or because of the call Natalie had gotten about a possible job there? But she hadn't said any more about it after the call from her agent.

"I'll think I'll be accepted by my peer group," he said. *Except maybe Natalie.* But she wouldn't be among the parents from the church's couples and singles groups taking the kids to Saratoga Springs for the Polar Express train ride tonight.

"What do you mean *peers*? We haven't had that word on our vocabulary list at school."

"The other adults, parents. I think I'll be okay with my pajama decision." *And pray I will with my job decision.*

"If you say so." Hope's skepticism was obvious. "I wonder who we'll sit with. The website says we'll be assigned seats."

Hope was a font of information. Connor wondered how much time Jared and Becca let her spend on the internet. She *was* only seven.

"I had Becca go over everything with me this afternoon, so I'd feel more con-fi-dent. That word hasn't been on our vocabulary list, either, but I heard Jared and Becca saying I was becoming more confident, so I asked my teacher what it means."

Connor's heart went out to the little girl. She'd been through so much, losing her mother and caretaker grandmother, and his father having abandoned her as he had Connor and his mother and brothers. Anyone would be insecure.

"I hope it's someone I know," Hope said. "Ari and Brendon aren't coming because their uncle, Becca's brother, and cousins are here. Alex and Sophia Hazard are, but they're more Ari's friends than mine. They're a grade ahead of me. I didn't ask anyone at Sunday school, except the big girls, Aimee and Amelia. They were helping Mrs. Hill with my class last Sunday."

After their stunt at the parsonage decorating, Aimee and Amelia weren't at the top of his list of people to socialize with, although they had gotten him and Natalie together in a way.

Hope chattered on. "They said they weren't coming. They're too big. But they aren't, really. You're bigger than they are and you're coming. Their mom and dad are bringing Robbie. He's little, not in school yet."

Andie must be feeling better. And Rob must have taken his suggestion that he do more with the kids to take some of the pressure off his wife. Connor hadn't been sure he'd gotten his point across when he'd talked with Rob on Sunday. But Rob had been so worried about Andie and lost as to how to help that he may have only appeared resistant to his counsel.

"I know we'll be seated with someone from church. I got that information when I called the Polar Express ticket office and set up for our group to come. Besides, you get to sit with me. What more could you want?"

"True. You won't get talking to the other grown-ups and forget about me?"

Connor stopped short in front of the door to the church hall and squatted to Hope's level. "Definitely not." He hugged her. "You're my date. I can't think of anyone who will be on the train ride that I'd rather be with than you."

A rap sounded on her bedroom door. "Hurry, Aunt Natalie."

Mom had said she'd keep Robbie downstairs with her while she got ready. Leave it to Andie to wait until the last possible minute to decide that she and Rob really did have the bug that Robbie had the other week. Natalie threw off her exasperation. She knew Andie and Rob didn't want to disappoint Robbie. Besides, taking the Polar Express again sounded like fun.

"I'm almost ready." She looked in the mirror with great reservations about her fashion choice. Her sweatshirt was emblazoned with Santa and his sleigh, complete with a red blinking nose on Rudolph. She'd received it as a gag gift at last year's holiday party at the TV station. Robbie had insisted she had to wear her pajamas just like him, and the sweatshirt and green yoga pants were the closest she could come for public display.

"We don't want to be late and miss the train," Robbie said through the door.

She opened it for him. "We won't miss the train." She slipped in earrings with Christmas bells that jingled when she moved her head, then dabbed on some red lip gloss.

"I like your pajamas. Does Grandma let you sleep in them with the light flashing?"

Natalie laughed. "No, I can turn the light off." She pressed the button sewn into the band at the bottom of the shirt.

"My pajamas aren't Christmas pajamas. They're Lego pajamas because I like Legos."

"So I see. Let's go downstairs and put our boots and coats on so we can get to church for our ride to the train station."

Since her mother's car was at Hill's garage for servicing, Natalie's father drove them to the church in his truck. Robbie chatted nonstop for the whole fifteen minutes. He was such a little person. Natalie hadn't spent any time with kids since college vacations when she sometimes babysat the twins. Her close work friends, if she could really count any as close, didn't have children. She could see how Andie and her older brother Marc, Claire's twin, got such joy out of being parents. Natalie hadn't thought about having kids of her own since high school…college…since she and Connor were together. She stared out the window at the dark starless night.

"Give me a call when you leave Saratoga," her father said as he braked to a stop in front of the door to the church hall, "and I'll be here to pick you up. Unless you get a better offer," he teased.

"Thanks. We might be able to catch a ride home with someone so you don't have to come out again."

"You could come on the Polar Express, too, Grandpa," Robbie said as he unbuckled from his booster seat. "We have Daddy's ticket."

"Thanks, bud, but I need to stay home in case Grandma needs my help."

Robbie nodded solemnly as he hopped out of the car. "Aunt Natalie and I will tell you all about it when you pick us up."

"I can't wait to hear."

"You'll wait up for us?" Robbie asked as Natalie unbuckled and removed his booster seat.

Her father chuckled. "I think we can stay up until eight."

"You can always rest your eyes in your chair." Robbie cited her father's favorite euphemism for dozing off in front of the TV.

She opened the door to the church hall for Robbie, welcoming the warmth after the short but bitter cold walk from the car. Robbie danced around beside her as she placed the booster seat along the wall and scanned the room. Her gaze hit Connor like a car skidding into a brick wall. What was he doing here? She wasn't expecting, wasn't prepared, to see him until church tomorrow morning. And she was wearing her silly reindeer sweatshirt.

"Aunt Natalie." Robbie grabbed her hand and hopped from foot to foot. "I forgot to go to the bathroom before we left Grandma's."

She could deal with seeing Connor here later. Right now she had a more immediate problem. Natalie scooped up Robbie and raced to the restrooms. She reached for the women's room doorknob.

"That's the girls' room," Robbie said.

"It's okay. I'll go in with you."

"No." He wiggled himself out of her arms to the floor and darted across the hall to the men's room. He opened the door and went in.

Natalie started in after him, but stopped when she heard voices inside. Robbie was four. He could handle his coat zipper and stuff, couldn't he? She had no idea. All she could think about was when she was about Robbie's age and had an accident at Autumn's house because she couldn't undo the clasps on her overalls.

"Come here often?" Connor lifted an eyebrow and tilted his head from her to the men's room door.

Natalie tossed her glove at his head.

He reached up, intercepted it and handed the glove to back to her. "Want me to go in and see if Robbie needs any help? I saw you race across the room."

"Yes, please." Leaning against the wall with a sigh of relief, she noticed Hope standing half behind her brother.

"And could you take Hope in for a pit stop?"

Connor was here with his little sister. They must be going on the train ride, too.

"Connor," Hope admonished. "This isn't a race."

"I think it was for Robbie." Connor ducked into the men's room with a chuckle.

"Connor is funny sometimes," Hope said.

Natalie was pretty sure the little girl meant odd, not humorous. "He can be." That was one of the many things Natalie liked about him. He could keep you on your toes. She pushed the door open for Hope and combed her hair while she waited for the little girl.

"Are you combing your hair to look pretty for Connor?" Hope asked. "He needs a helpmate, you know. That's like a wife. Mrs. Hill said so."

Natalie choked. "My hat mussed my hair." She was *not* combing her hair for Connor. "Do you want me to comb yours?"

Hope looked in the mirror. "No, I'm good. Connor brushed it and put my barrettes in for me before we left his house." The little girl sized her up. "You might make a good wife for Connor. Amelia and Aimee said you're a TV person. If Connor was sick, you wouldn't be afraid to stand up in front of church and do his sermon for him."

Natalie doubted she'd be anyone's first choice to sub for Connor at church. Before she could even start to respond to Hope, the little girl confided, "I don't like talking or reading in front of people, except I read out loud for Becca to practice my reading. I'm glad we don't have show-and-tell in first grade."

"I can tell you my secret for not being afraid to talk in front of people."

"What?"

"I pretend I'm talking to someone I'm close to like my m—" Natalie stopped herself before she said mother "—sister Claire."

"I don't have any sisters. But I have three brothers.

Connor is the best listener. I could pretend I'm talking to him."

"Connor's a good choice," Natalie said. "When we were friends in school, sometimes I practiced my book reports for him before I had to give them in class. If he was in my class, I looked in his direction and gave my report like I was talking just to him."

"You guys have must have been friends for a long time." Hope looked up at her, hands on hips. "Have you thought about marrying him?"

Natalie swallowed her surprise and regret. *Only too often for my own good, little one.*

Connor stared at the closed door. What was taking Natalie and Hope so long?

Drew Stacey, Autumn's uncle and the current leader of the church's couples group, called for everyone to start organizing into their car-pool groups.

"Pastor Connor," Robbie said, biting his lip. "If everyone else leaves without us, you'll drive us to the train station so we don't miss the Polar Express, won't you? Grandpa drove us. Aunt Natalie doesn't have a car."

"Sure, I can drive us." He'd planned on Hope and him riding in the church van, but he could run over and get his car. That might be a better idea anyway. It would free up more seats in the van for others. And give him and Natalie some unexpected time together. He lifted his hand to knock on the door and hit air when it opened.

"What took you guys so long?" Robbie voiced Connor's earlier thought.

"Natalie had to comb her hair because her hat messed it up," Hope answered.

Connor's chest swelled a little. He was pretty sure the pink on Natalie's cheeks wasn't makeup.

"But she didn't have to comb mine because you already did it good, Connor. We also had a girl talk."

The strangled look on Natalie's face made Connor eager to hear more.

"I'm not going to tell you what we said because it was just for us girls."

Connor saw the relief spread through Natalie, making him even more curious. "Drew just called for everyone to organize into their car-pool groups."

"We're supposed to ride in the van. Robbie's car seat is over by the door."

"Us, too. Jared dropped off Hope's seat here before he brought her over," Connor said, deciding to offer to drive them instead. "But I—"

"Hey, Connor," Drew called as he strode across the room. "Can you drive yourself and a couple other people?" He eyed Natalie and Robbie, smiling. "We seem to have more people going than we have room for in the van and cars."

"No problem. The four of us were all going to ride in the church van. Does that give you enough seats? I could fit one more person."

"No," Drew said, "that'll do it. Thanks." He went back to organizing the others.

"Looks like I will be driving, Robbie."

Natalie shot him a questioning look.

"Robbie was concerned everyone was going to leave and you don't have a car." It struck Connor that he'd totally acted for Natalie without asking her first. "You don't mind riding with us, do you?"

"No, of course not," she answered so quickly that he

couldn't tell if he'd irritated her by not asking first or if she wanted to ride with them.

"I've got to run back to the parsonage and get the car. Hope and I walked over."

"Okay."

"Hope, you stay with Natalie. I'll be right back."

The little girl nodded.

Connor couldn't help strutting across the hall. Without looking, he knew that Natalie was watching him. He whistled Christmas carols while he jogged back to the parsonage.

The hour drive to Saratoga Springs flew by, with the kids' excitement escalating the closer they got.

"I hope we get to sit with you, Natalie," Hope said as they entered the train depot and found the rest of the group. "We have assigned seats, like at school." The little girl craned her neck to look around. "I don't see any of my other friends here."

"I'd like that, too," Natalie said. "I don't see any of my close friends either."

"Except Connor," Hope said.

Connor's ears perked up. *Maybe that's what the two of them had been talking about at the church hall— Natalie and me being friends.* Seemed like a good sign to him. Maybe if they weren't officially seated together, he could get Natalie and Robbie's seatmates to switch with him and Hope. He glanced at Natalie. But this time he'd ask first.

"Nat." He motioned to her. She stepped closer, cocking her head. "Would you mind if I tried to change our seating so you and Robbie are seated with us? Everyone is in groups of four. For Hope," he added. "She seems to have warmed to you. She doesn't to everyone."

"I guess. I wouldn't want to upset her like I did at the parsonage decorating."

Not exactly the resounding yes he'd like, but he'd take it. "I'll talk with Drew and find out who's seated where. You'll keep an eye on Hope?"

Natalie nodded.

"Hope." It took the little girl a moment to realize Connor was talking to her.

"Everything here is so pretty," she said.

"It is. I need to go talk with Mr. Stacey. Natalie will stay here with you."

"Okay." Her gaze went back to the glittery Christmas decorations.

He wove his way across the depot to where the Staceys were standing. "Drew, I need a favor."

"Let me guess," his wife, Emily, said. "You and Natalie want to sit together. I've been watching the two of you," she added with a twinkle in her eye.

He couldn't escape it. For a fleeting moment, he was ready to text his friend that he would take the assistant pastor job in Chicago. It would be refreshing to serve somewhere where everyone didn't know all his business, past and present.

"It's for Hope. She'd like Natalie to sit with us."

"Mmm-hmm," Emily said.

Connor looked at Drew for help.

"I can't do anything with her," he said. "But I can see who's lined up to sit with Natalie and Robbie." Drew glanced down at the paper he held. "It's Neal and Ian."

Emily grinned at the mention of her older brother and nephew.

"No problem," Drew said. "Not only am I doing you

a favor, but this will get me points with my mother-in-law, too."

"Yeah," Emily added. "After practice last Tuesday, Mom was saying how you and Natalie make a cute couple."

Connor groaned. *Mary Hazard, too?* He could make a lot of his parishioners happy if he could convince Natalie to give things another go. But they wouldn't be his parishioners anymore if he took the Chicago job. He dismissed the pall that thought cast. "I owe you, Drew."

"And I'll remember that when we're opening camp next summer. I'm sure I can find something for you to lend a hand with."

If he was here next summer.

"Here are the seat numbers for you and Natalie and the kids."

Him and Natalie and the kids. Drew's words hit Connor in a spot inside him that he'd kept closed off. The spot that used to house his dreams of having a life, a family with Natalie.

"When they call us to board the train, you can go ahead without checking in with me."

"Good, and thanks." Connor returned to Natalie.

"Is there a problem?" she asked.

Connor softened his expression. "No. I was checking things with Drew. He gave me our seat numbers."

"Who are we sitting with?" Hope asked.

"Natalie and Robbie. Just like you wanted."

"Goody," she said.

"That wouldn't happen to have anything to do with what you had to check with Drew?" Natalie asked with a knowing smile.

"It turns out Hope and me changing seats helps Drew out, too."

"How's that?"

The playful tone of Natalie's question took him back to earlier times, when they were completely comfortable with each other.

"Now I owe him a favor that he's promised to call in when it's time to open Sonrise camp for next year's summer season."

Her smile dipped. Was she thinking about her not being in Paradox Lake next summer or him still being here?

"All aboard," a deep voice blasted across the depot. "All board for the Polar Express."

"It's time to go." Hope jumped up and down next to him.

"Come on, Aunt Natalie," Robbie said, grabbing her hand.

Connor took Hope's hand and placed his other hand on the small of Natalie's back to guide the group out of the depot to the waiting train. Next summer was months away. For now, he wasn't going to worry about the future, just take joy in being with Natalie today.

When they reached the train, he dropped his hand and let Robbie and Natalie board ahead of him and Hope. Stepping up into the train, Natalie looked back over her shoulder. She gave him a smile that rivaled the kids' grins in pure happiness and filled him with hope. Nothing that felt this strong and right could be all one-sided. He lifted Hope onto the train step and bounded up after her. This time he wasn't going to let geography, Natalie's doubts about herself and her life, or anything else get in the way of them having a life together.

Chapter Eleven

Natalie punched her pillow, rolled over for what seemed like the hundredth time and tried to go back to sleep. She'd let down her guard with Connor and the kids yesterday, ignoring her intention to keep him at a distance so he wouldn't read more in to their relationship than friendship. The minute she closed her eyes, her head filled with pictures of him smiling and laughing, remembrances of his every random touch, the caring way he'd treated her.

She feared she'd led him on as she had in college, let him think they had the future they were playing at yesterday with Hope and Robbie. What else could he think? She'd gotten caught up in the moment and the Christmas spirit. She'd even agreed to help him host the open house at the parsonage today.

She tossed over again. No, she hadn't led Connor on. She'd simply given up keeping her feelings bottled inside. When those feelings had escaped, all the barriers she'd put up to keep Connor at a distance had crumbled. She had to accept the truth. She was in love with him. Not the childish love of their high school years or even what she'd felt for him in college. An all-out "we're in this for life" love. And she had no idea what she was going to do about it. With her self-admission, Natalie fell back into a deeper sleep for a couple of hours until the jingle of a bell in the hall woke her again. Robbie and the bell he'd gotten on the Polar Express ride. She glanced at the clock. Six forty-five.

Natalie jumped out of bed. She hadn't heard Dad and Paul get up to do chores. She threw on a robe and slippers and covered the steps to the door in three seconds, hoping to stop Robbie before he woke up her mother. That is, if her mother hadn't already gotten up to make Dad and Paul breakfast.

"Hi, Aunt Natalie," Robbie said when she cracked the door open. "I'm being a Christmas alarm clock."

"And doing a great job of it. But let's let Grandma and Aunt Claire sleep a while longer." She scooted the little boy downstairs to the kitchen, where she found a lukewarm pot of coffee sitting in the coffeemaker and two mugs in the sink, but no other dishes. The guys must have gone out to do chores without breakfast.

"What do you say we make everybody chocolate-chip pancakes for breakfast? Grandpa and Uncle Paul will be hungry when they get in from chores."

"Goody. I can help?"

"Of course." Natalie moved the stepping stool over to the kitchen counter from its place next to the broom closet.

"Mommy lets me help her, even though Aimee and Amelia say I'm too little."

Natalie gave Robbie a cup of flour to pour into the bowl. "I know how that is. Your mommy and Uncle Marc and Aunt Claire are all older than I am, and they used to say the same thing."

"When I'm big, I'm going to help Daddy with the cows like Uncle Paul does. I only get to help feed the baby cows sometimes." He turned his big brown eyes to Natalie, his mouth set in a serious expression. "Can I tell you a secret?"

She regrasped the milk carton so it wouldn't slip out of her hand, not sure she wanted to know any more of Robbie's family's secrets.

The little boy didn't wait for her to answer. "I'm kind of afraid of the big cows. You won't tell my sisters, will you?"

"Never."

"My mommy is afraid of mice, so I can't get a gerbil, but Daddy isn't afraid of anything."

Natalie poured the milk into the bowl. She knew better than to counter her nephew on that one, although she knew her brother-in-law had been frightened by Andie's anxiety attack. "Do you want to stir?"

"Yep." He took the wooden spoon and swirled the ingredients together. "Are you afraid of anything?"

Aside from the strength of her love for Connor and making another mistake with him? She cleared her throat. "I'm afraid of driving on snowy roads."

"Then it's a good thing we went to the Polar Express with Pastor Connor. 'Cause the roads were snowy when he drove us home."

"Yes, they were. I'm glad he drove us, too." *And glad I got to spend the day with him and that he's come back into my life and that God seems to be showing me we can have a future.*

Robbie gave the pancake batter another swirl. "I think it's time for chocolate chips."

"You're right. Good job." She handed him the open bag of chocolate chips.

He dumped them in and stirred, his expression turning thoughtful. "Is Pastor Connor your boyfriend? He was holding your hand when we got off the Polar Express. Amelia holds hands with her boyfriend. I've seen them in the hall at Sunday school."

Natalie choked.

"Aimee and Amelia said Pastor Connor likes you. You should ask him to be your boyfriend. That's what Amelia did."

"Good call, sport."

Natalie spun around to see Claire in the kitchen doorway. She walked over and ruffled their nephew's hair.

"So, Nat, what do you say? You going to do it?"

Natalie's heart pounded at the thought. But, yes, she'd do it. Ask him *something* like that. Today. At the open house.

Her determination had waned by that afternoon, when she pulled her father's truck into Connor's empty driveway. Her parents would be coming later with Claire in her car. Although the open house wouldn't start for almost an hour, she'd expected some of the church women to be here setting up. She checked the dashboard clock. Connor had pulled her aside at coffee hour after church and asked her to come over about one. It was five after.

When she stepped out of the truck, the north wind stung her cheeks and legs. Her leather boots slipped on the icy driveway. What had possessed her to wear them and a dress, instead of her Columbia snow boots and wool slacks or jeans? Vanity, pure and simple. She knew the dress flattered her, and the boots were a confidence booster. She'd worn them on all her successful job interviews. But the open house wasn't exactly a job interview. It wasn't as if she was applying to be the pastor's wife.

She shook that whole silly line of thought out of her head as she minced her way to the front door, where Connor was waiting. Anxious to see her? Nervous about the open house? She scanned his handsome face. He appeared as relaxed as can be. A gentle smile curved his lips.

"Hey," he said, holding the door open for her. "I'm glad you're here."

She stomped the snow off her boots, hoping he'd see the pink on her cheeks as windburn and not warmth from his welcome.

"Karen Hill and the other women dropped off all the food after church. I told them I could handle the setup. But there are some appetizer things that need to be cooked in the oven. I'm basically a microwave type of guy, and there's a note on them that says don't microwave."

The bubble of warmth surrounding her deflated. He was glad to see her for her help.

"Hand me your coat, and I'll hang it up."

As she unbuttoned her coat, she ran her gaze over him, rethinking her clothing choice. Connor was dressed much more casually than she was in well-washed jeans and a red bulky-knit cotton sweater that fell softly from his broad shoulders. An advertisement for a man comfortable entertaining at home. Except the way he was practically bouncing on the balls of his feet gave him away.

He hung her coat in the entryway closet and motioned

to a coatrack to the right side of the door. "I brought the rack over from the church for the guests' coats."

Natalie squelched an urge to hug herself. It was no big deal that he'd put her coat in his closet, rather than hanging it on the rack. He probably wanted to make more room for the guests' coats.

"Now, I need you in the kitchen, woman." Connor walked her through the living room.

She stopped in front of the Christmas tree, her throat clogging. "You put the star on top."

"Yes, I did. Hope helped me after we got back yesterday."

Natalie blinked her eyes against the blurred colors of the tree lights. Had Connor felt the same change in their relationship yesterday that she had?

"I like it," she said.

Connor grabbed her hand and tugged her toward the dining room. "You'll have lots of time to admire the tree later when everyone is here. For now, we have some cooking to do in the kitchen."

"Lead on." She entwined her fingers in his, enjoying the quirk of a smile she received when she did.

After she'd put the mini quiche appetizers in the oven and set the stove timer, she and Connor got to work placing the donated food on the dining room table and sideboard.

"Hey," she said, slapping Connor's hand after he'd snatched a third snickerdoodle from the generous platter of cookies Autumn's grandmother had made. "Save some of those for the guests. If you sample this much at all of the church functions, you'll weigh three hundred pounds by the time you've been here five years."

His eyes darkened with emotion. The shadow of the

thought that he might not be here, where he was so obviously happy and comfortable, in five years? Maybe not be here because of her? She touched her fingertips to her lips. But Claire and Autumn had both insisted Connor wouldn't take the position in Chicago or do anything else he didn't want to do. Her chest tightened. Did they know him better than she did now?

He patted his almost-concave stomach. "Not a chance. I have good metabolism and a membership at the gym in Ticonderoga."

"Eek!" Something brushed against Natalie's ankle, breaking her focus on Connor.

"You don't believe me?" Connor teased.

"No," she answered, hopping on one foot. "There's something under the table."

He lifted the tablecloth and bent over, his sweater stretching across his broad back. When he stood, he held a snarling, hissing, half-grown, orange-striped cat.

"You have a cat," she said, stating the obvious.

He held the animal away from him. "Yes and no. It's more like the cat has me."

She laughed. "That's usually the case with cats."

Apparently reconsidering the situation, the cat rubbed his ear against Connor's arm. He drew it closer and tentatively petted it. "It's a stray that's been hanging out in the garage off and on for the past couple of weeks. I've been leaving out food, trying to catch it so I can take it to the shelter, in case someone is looking for him…her. It must have come in when people were bringing the food in after church."

"Friendly little guy," Natalie said, reaching toward the feline.

The cat stopped its purring, raised a paw, claws out, and hissed.

"It has to be a girl," Natalie said, snatching her hand back.

The cat backed off and rubbed Connor's arm again for more petting.

"Why do you say that?" he asked.

"She's jealous and protecting her ownership." *Just as I would*, Natalie realized, the thought bringing back the resolution she'd made after talking with Robbie and Claire this morning to let Connor know her feelings.

"So, you're jealous, are you, little one?" Connor said in a rumbly voice that released a flock of butterflies inside her. She shifted her gaze from the cat to Connor's face and caught a teasing sparkle in his eyes. Did he remember what that voice did to her?

The stove timer sounded.

"The mini quiches are done." She brushed by Connor and the cat to get them. As Natalie bent over the open oven door, she heard his footsteps behind her. She stood there for a few extra moments, letting the heat rise, hoping Connor would attribute the flush on her face to the warm kitchen air. She hadn't blushed this much since middle school. Natalie lifted the cookie sheet to the stove top and grabbed the spatula hanging on the wall behind the stove. "Do you have a platter I could put them on?"

He reached over her shoulder and opened the upper cupboard next to the stove. "Like this?" he asked, looking pleased with himself as he placed a large floral-patterned plate on the counter.

"Perfect." She began moving the appetizers from the pan to the plate and stopped. She looked around the kitchen. "Where's the kitten?"

"I left her in the living room."

"Do you think that's safe?" She turned to face him and caught his gaze fixed on her, a soft gleam in his eyes. When had he moved so close?

"About as safe as I am here alone with you." Connor lifted the spatula from her hand, placed it next to the platter and pushed a stray curl off her cheek. He lowered his face to hers.

The front door opened and slammed shut to the tune of multiple footsteps. "Hey, Ginger, get down or you'll knock the star off the tree." Hope's words shot through Natalie. She started to jump back, but Connor's strong arms stopped her, pulling her away from the stove and back toward him.

"The hot stove," he said.

The oven was closed and not hot enough to be a danger, but Natalie gave herself a moment to enjoy being in his embrace. "We'd better get into the other room."

"Yeah." He slowly disengaged his arms.

The kitchen door swung in and Hope raced over. "Connor, you have to come. Your kitty climbed the tree and is trying to knock the star off."

"My kitty?"

"Yes, the one you said is a stray that you put food out in the garage for. When I come over, I've been teaching her not to be afraid to come in the house. I know having a new family can be scary."

Natalie teared up a little at Hope's serious tone and expression.

"I named her Ginger. I thought she could be my Christmas present to you. Then you wouldn't be alone here all of the time, except when I come for sleepovers."

Connor exchanged a glance with Natalie; the soft look

on his face for his sister made Natalie's limbs melt. She had to tell him how she felt before she left today.

They followed the little girl into the other room, where Jared was attempting to separate the cat from the Christmas tree branches. "Ouch." The cat scratched the top of his hand and he dropped her to the floor. "Where did you get that little spitfire?"

Connor's face split into a grin. "Evidently, she's our sister's Christmas gift to me."

Jared lifted his hands in surrender. "We had no part of this." He motioned between his wife, Becca, and himself.

"It was going to be a surprise, but Connor let her inside before I could tell him."

"No, I didn't let her in. I think she must have come in with one of the people dropping off food this morning."

"So she chose you to be her family, like I was teaching her to." Hope bubbled with excitement.

Like my heart is telling me to, Natalie thought.

As if to acknowledge Hope, the kitten walked over to Connor and rubbed against his legs so he'd pick her up. She started purring the moment he did, garnering a lifted eyebrow from his brother.

"We Donnelly brothers do have a way with the ladies," Jared said, wrapping his arm around Becca's waist. He laughed as he eyed Connor and the cat. "Just different ladies."

"We need to finish the appetizers in the kitchen," Natalie reminded Connor, ignoring the frown that spread across Jared's face as he looked from Connor to her. If she got Connor back in the kitchen, she could tell him, even with his family in the other room. Tell him before she lost her nerve and came up with reasons not to. And if things didn't go as she hoped, she could put on her professional face, mingle and chat with the open house guests when they started arriving and, after a reasonable amount of time, escape home.

A rap sounded on the front door.

"Go ahead and get it," Becca said. "I'll help Natalie in the kitchen."

"Okay, thanks." Connor bounded to the door.

Natalie's heart sank at his eager response to answer the door rather than help her in the kitchen. She was being juvenile. He was only doing his job, not rejecting her. "I can handle things in the kitchen," she said. She didn't want to be rude, but Becca had been her high school history teacher and she was a little uncomfortable socializing with her. Besides, she needed to be alone to regroup. "Go ahead and enjoy yourself," she added and waved at the food-laden table in the dining room as if she was Connor's hostess.

For the rest of the afternoon she and Connor worked side-by-side, welcoming and talking with the open house guests and replenishing the refreshment table. More than once, she'd thought, *So this is how it would feel if I was the pastor's wife.* And even more often, she wished the crowd would thin and the open house would be over, so she could have few minutes of time alone with Connor to talk before she lost her nerve.

Connor listened with half an ear to Tom Hill explaining what he had to do to the church van to get it to pass the state vehicle inspection. The real focus of his attention was on Natalie, as it had been all afternoon. She puzzled him. In some ways, she'd seemed more relaxed, helping him as if that was what she was meant to do and mixing with the guests. But she also had an aura of tension around her.

"If the work needs to be done, we'll have to have it done," he said at the appropriate time in the conversation. "We use the van a lot. Check with Ted Hazard about the payment. He's the church treasurer."

"I'm not worried about being paid," Tom said. "Just letting you know what needs to be done. I'll go ahead with the work and have the van back in commission tomorrow or Tuesday."

"By Tuesday would be great. We have dress rehearsal for the pageant and offered transportation to anyone who needed it. I have some standby car-pool offers, but the van would be more convenient."

"No problem," Tom said.

Through the archway, Connor caught sight of Natalie's mouth drawing into a grim line. She was in a small group on the other side of the living room with Jared, Josh and Claire. "Excuse me," he said. "There's someone I need to catch in the other room." That someone being Jared. He hadn't gotten any sign from his brother that his opinion of Natalie had changed since their conversation when she'd first returned. And Josh had been all about Connor not getting serious with her, or any woman from what he could tell from Josh.

"I disagree," Natalie responded to something Josh said as Connor approached.

He clenched his fists and closed the remaining distance between him and Natalie. The guys had better back off. As casually as he could, he slipped his arm around Natalie and rested his hand at her waist, deriving satisfaction from both her accepting his action and the dark look Jared gave him.

"I think you can present the news in a positive and objective way," she said.

He relaxed. They were talking work.

"At the last station I worked for, I was part of a segment called 'Good News Today' that reported on uplifting, positive local news."

Connor shifted his weight, realizing how little he knew about Natalie's television work.

"Right," Josh said, "but those were feel-good stories you went in search of. We're talking the real everyday news."

Leave it to Josh to find a down spin.

When Jared nodded in agreement, Connor's brain went into fast retrieval mode to come up with something solid to refute his brothers and support Natalie.

She was faster. "The world is an ugly place sometimes, and some of that ugly has to be reported. But I don't see any reason that ugliness can't be balanced with positive, inspiring stories and commentary from all sides of the opinion spectrum. One thing I learned back in your wife's senior public affairs class, Jared, is that sometimes you have to listen to all sides, the truth and the lies, to get the real facts."

He puffed with pride for Natalie. The woman was good.

She smiled up at him. He hadn't said that out loud, had he? No, his brothers wouldn't have let that get by without a comment.

"Doesn't God encourage us to spread the good news, to help drive out the evil?" she asked.

"What's your professional take on that, little brother?" Jared asked.

Connor pressed his lips together as he thought. Was she stretching things? "I think Natalie has a valid point."

Both Jared and Josh smirked as if they'd expected his response and were dismissing his statement.

That didn't stop him. "We all have our callings. Broadcasting inspirational, positive, what you called feel-good stories, Josh, can show the Lord's hand in things. 'Spread the good news,' as Natalie said. Objective reporting of other news shows the evil that exists in our world. Evil we should combat every day." He knew he was sermonizing, but he didn't care. That was part of what he was called to do. And, if it supported Natalie, all the better.

"I see what you mean," Claire said, offering her first contribution to the conversation since he'd joined them. He wasn't sure if she meant him or Natalie or both of them. But he appreciated her support.

Natalie nodded, excitement shining in her eyes that he'd understood her. He wanted to hug her to his side, but his arm around her was as much of a public show as he dared make, especially since he wasn't sure exactly where he and Natalie stood.

"Thank you, Pastor Connor," Josh said.

Connor almost expected mock applause from him. "Jared asked for my professional opinion."

Jared looked pensive. "I need to think that over."

Connor preened at his oldest brother's marginal concession. If only he could get as much of one from him about Natalie. Not that what Jared or anyone else thought of her would make him love her any less. But if he had his way, Natalie was going to be family.

"Mom's waving to me," Claire said. "They're probably ready to leave." She left the group, followed by Josh.

Connor's stomach clenched. Josh wasn't putting the moves on Natalie's sister, was he? The thought disturbed him more than it should. Claire and Josh were both adults.

Natalie touched his arm. "Thanks for helping me with your brothers."

"You were doing okay on your own, but that's what friends are for."

"Is that what we are? Friends?"

Natalie's inflection made her question sound like being friends wasn't a good thing. Before he could pursue that thought, several people descended on Natalie and him to thank him for opening up the parsonage to the public.

"I'm glad you could come," he said to one couple. "I hope to see you at the ecumenical Christmas pageant," he told a family who had recently moved to the Paradox Lake area and were church shopping. "It's at seven o'clock Saturday evening at the Sonrise Camp auditorium." Soon, the living room was empty except for Tom and Karen Hill…and Josh. He glanced toward the dining room, looking for Natalie. She couldn't—*wouldn't*—have slipped out while he was saying goodbye to everyone. He took a half step toward the other room.

"That went well, didn't it?" Karen asked from behind him.

For a split second, he toyed with the idea of pretending he hadn't heard her so he could go and see if Natalie was in the kitchen. But he shut out the temptation, rising above his adolescent-like need for reassurance that Nat hadn't left. She was either still here or she wasn't. Taking a minute to talk with Karen and Tom wouldn't change that either way.

He pasted a smile on his face. "Not bad at all."

"See, I told you it would be easy. And Natalie was a big help. You two make a good team."

Connor shoved his fingers in the front pockets of his jeans. He thought so, too, but he didn't want Karen, his parishioners, thinking there was any more to his and Natalie's relationship than her helping out today—at least not until he knew for sure where they stood.

"Do you want us to stay and help you guys clean up?" Karen asked.

"No, we've got it," Josh answered before Connor had a chance.

"Hey, Connor," Claire called from the dining room as she walked through it to join them. "Natalie needs your help in the kitchen."

So, Claire's still here and, better, so is Nat. Connor controlled the urge to break into a grin.

"Looks like you're all set," Karen said with a twinkle in her eye. "Go." She waved toward the kitchen. "We'll let ourselves out."

Connor glanced from Josh to Claire. As difficult as it was, he held his pace to a saunter until he was out of their sight.

Natalie was standing in the kitchen, leaning against the counter, with an atypical look of uncertainty on her face.

His heart skipped two beats. From the tone of Claire's voice, he was expecting something good. Natalie's expression didn't exactly confirm that. "What's up?"

"I have to tell you something."

Her words weren't any more reassuring than her expression.

"I want to be more than friends."

His heart picked up the two missed beats and then some.

She scuffed her boot on the vinyl floor, releasing a huff of disgust. "Let me try again. That sounded so juvenile."

"No need." He held his arms out to her, and Natalie stepped into them. "For me," he whispered into her hair, "we've always been more than friends."

"Even when I treated you so badly in college?"

"Even then. But we were young and didn't know what we wanted."

She nodded against his shoulder.

Now, with her words, he had exactly what he wanted. What he'd always wanted. A future with Natalie. He hugged her tight. No power on earth could make him let her slip away again.

Chapter Twelve

"Tomorrow at nine. I'll be there." Natalie could barely contain her excitement as she hung up then pressed the internet icon on her phone to find a flight to Chicago. She tapped her fingernail on the screen while she waited and prayed out loud, "Thank You, Lord, for giving me this opportunity, and that the research farm let Claire take this week off in lieu of her annual bonus, so she can help Mom." A popular travel site loaded. *Wait until I tell Connor.*

Her excitement dropped a notch as she thought about the open house yesterday and dress rehearsal for the pageant tonight. She brushed it off. The other day, Connor had sounded serious about considering the job offer he had from his friend in the Chicago area. And Andie could substitute for her tonight.

Yes. Her search showed an early evening flight from Burlington, Vermont, so she wouldn't need to have someone drive her all of the way to Albany. And it wasn't too outrageously expensive. Natalie calculated in her head whether the long-overdue security deposit refund she received last week from her last apartment's management company would cover the cost. It was close. She punched in her debit card number and held her breath. The charge went through. She lifted a finger to call Connor and stopped. This was information better shared in person.

She made a quick explanation to her mother that she needed to run over to the church to talk with Connor, without saying why, and asked Claire if she could borrow her car. It was worth putting up with the knowing smiles she received from both of them. She wanted Connor to be the first to know. She flew out of the house and had to keep lifting her foot off the gas pedal to stay within the speed limit on the drive to the church. When she stopped the car in the parking lot, she waited a moment and breathed in and out a couple of times to contain her excitement. Then she hurried into the church and down the hall to Connor's office. The door was shut, and she could hear the hum of voices. She shook her hands and paced the hall until she heard the turn of the doorknob.

"Thanks for bringing the van back," Connor said. "Do you need a lift home?"

"No." Tom Hill's response came through the crack of the door. "Jack said he'd swing by on his way back from the hardware store in Schroon Lake. He should be here by now."

Natalie hadn't noticed anyone in the parking lot, but she'd been in such a rush to see Connor that she could have missed Jack's truck sitting right in front of her.

"If he's not there, come back in," Connor said. "I'm here for another hour and don't have any appointments scheduled."

Tom pushed the door open and smiled hello when

he saw Natalie. "Looks like you have an unscheduled one, though."

"Hi, Tom," she said. "Like Connor said, if Jack isn't here, come back in. You won't be interrupting. I just have some news I wanted to share." She hoped her words sounded more gracious than she felt.

Tom grabbed his gloves from his coat pocket and pulled them on. "And Connor, you'll let us know about—" He stopped. "That other matter we discussed."

"I sure will," Connor said.

They watched Tom walk down the hall and out the front door.

"I thought he'd never leave," Connor said a minute later, when Tom didn't return, echoing her thoughts. He motioned her into his office. "After you."

She walked past him.

He followed and reached to close the door. "Uh, maybe I'd better leave the door open."

"Don't want to give your parishioners the wrong idea," she teased.

"You are definitely *not* the wrong idea."

Her heart pounded, either from the way his words warmed her or a fear that he'd change his mind once she told him her news. She didn't want him to think she was choosing her career over him again. Maybe coming over had been a bad idea. Seeing Connor here in his office with Tom brought back the same doubt she'd had earlier when she'd thought about Connor and her at the open house. The last thing she wanted to see was that look of hurt in Connor's eyes that was seared in her mind from the night she'd turned down his marriage proposal.

"So, what's up?" He pulled the chair by his desk out

for her. "Something about the pageant, or is this visit strictly social?"

The way he lifted his eyebrows with his last question evoked a nervous laugh from Natalie. "Actually, it's about dress rehearsal tonight, and I have some news."

Connor sat at his desk and leaned forward on his crossed arms, giving her his total attention.

She swallowed the lump in her throat. "I won't be able to make practice."

His eyes darkened.

Not the best start to sharing her good news.

"Is it your mother?" Concern laced his voice.

"No, Mom's good. Let me start over. I got a call this morning from the station manager about the job my agent told me about. The manager was the news director when I was there before. Kirk and the former station manager are gone." She searched his face for any change in his expression before continuing but didn't see even a flicker in his eyes. "The manager invited me to audition in a reality-TV-like competition for a spot as their new 'good news' reporter, like I did at my last station."

"And like we were talking about at the open house."

She shifted in her chair at his mention of the open house. "Right."

"That's great," he said, sounding genuinely happy for her.

Maybe he *was* seriously considering the job offer he had in the Chicago area, and she was worrying unnecessarily.

"But what does that have to do with the pageant?" he asked.

She drew a deep breath. "The station is holding the two-day audition blitz this week. The station management thinks the holiday season is the perfect time to introduce this new segment. My agent got me in just under the wire, probably only because the director knows me." Her words tumbled out at a staccato rate. "I booked a flight for early this evening."

"Oh." He straightened in his chair.

"Practice should be fine. Andie can fill in for me like Jared did for you last practice. The choir is more than ready."

He nodded. "When will you be back?"

"Late Friday, in plenty of time for the pageant Saturday evening."

The look of relief that passed over Connor's face flowed into her. She pushed back in her seat from the edge of the chair, where she'd worked herself to as she'd told Connor her plans.

"I'll pick you up from the airport."

"Making sure I don't bail on you?"

"I do like having you where I can keep an eye on you." He grinned.

Natalie breathed out slowly. His comic innuendo told her he was taking all of this okay. "I'm flying into Burlington, so you won't have to drive so far. Dad's taking me this evening."

Connor's cell phone dinged. He shut it down. "A calendar reminder. I'd invite you to catch some lunch with me, except I have a hospital visit in Saranac Lake and just enough time to get there."

"I'll take a rain check," she said. "Work is work."

His mouth curved down slightly, making her belatedly realize that Connor probably had many aspects of his job that he didn't see as work. One of the many things that made him a good small-town pastor. She corrected herself. A good pastor period.

Natalie pushed the chair back from the desk and stood. She knew she shouldn't ask about church business, but she couldn't stop herself. Getting the right answer would help dispel the niggling doubt about Connor and her interview that his frown had brought back. "Don't answer this if you can't."

He stood and wrinkled his forehead.

"Was the other matter Tom mentioned your contract renewal?" She shifted her weight from one foot to the other as she waited for Connor's answer.

"No. In July, the church will be celebrating the two hundredth anniversary of the original church formed here in the old Hazardtown hamlet that Hazardtown Community Church evolved from. The administrative council would like to publish a church history for the celebration. Tom thinks that because I write sermons, I'm a good candidate to write the history."

The way Connor leaned against the desk toward her gave him away. "You want to write it," she said.

"Yeah." He grinned and pushed away from the desk. "Although Becca might be a better choice." He grabbed his coat from the coat tree. "Not that I want to get rid of you, but I have to leave. Want to come?"

She wavered. "I can't. I have to get ready for tomorrow."

He walked her to her car and gave her a quick peck. "Break a leg tomorrow, or whatever it is I'm supposed to say."

"Thanks. I'll call you."

"You'd better."

Natalie watched him walk to his car, wishing she

could ride along with him for his hospital visit. She checked the car clock. There wouldn't be enough time. On her drive home, she tried to rekindle her initial excitement about the interview in Chicago. But all she could think about was the church history Connor wanted to write for the celebration in July, when she might be back working in Chicago.

Natalie hadn't called last night when she'd arrived in Chicago. He checked his cell phone again. Nor had she called this morning. He tossed the phone in his gym bag, shoved the bag in the locker and gave the combination lock a twirl. He'd thought about calling her but had refrained because she'd said she'd call. He didn't want to make her feel pressured, possibly interfere with her audition. Nor did he want to let on how needy he was to hear her voice. He headed directly to a weight bench. Some serious bench presses might be just what he needed to take the edge off waiting to hear from her.

He threw on twenty more pounds than he usually lifted. Natalie had been right, the pageant dress rehearsal last night had gone okay with Andie filling in for her. He pressed up and groaned. But that didn't mean that he wasn't nervous about her being gone. He brought the weights down. He knew he was prejudiced, but Andie wouldn't be as good at directing the choir. Nor was she as musically talented as Natalie, and not only in his opinion. If Natalie didn't return in time for the pageant, he feared it could flop, which might affect the administrative council's vote on his contract renewal. And he didn't want to let down his fellow pastors. But he couldn't build his life on fears—fears of the council not renewing his contract, fears that if he took his friend's offer, he'd be accepting it for the wrong reasons, fears that Natalie would choose her work over him again. They each needed to do whatever God wanted them to do. Connor acknowledged to himself that he had to focus on what His direction was, not what Connor wanted it to be. With that decision, he pressed the weights up hard and fast.

"Hey, bro, you should have told me yesterday you were going to work out this morning. We could have come together."

Connor let the weights slip down into the uprights with a bang. He sat up on the bench to face Josh. "I figured you'd be at work."

"I had to take a 'use it or lose it' vacation day. The boss lady doesn't like it if you don't take at least a certain number of your earned vacation days, and I haven't. I'm taking Christmas Eve and New Year's Eve, too." He dropped his gym bag on the bench beside Connor. "You'd think Anne would appreciate that I'd rather be at work than take vacation."

"News flash, Josh. There are more important things in life besides work." Connor's words resonated in his head. That's what he needed to pray about, how to balance all of the important things in his life.

"Such as women? You and Natalie were looking pretty tight at the open house."

For a split second, Connor considered confiding in his brother, but Josh's leering grin put a stop to that thought. He couldn't take his brother making fun of his feelings for Natalie. "Go change and I'll run a couple of laps with you."

"So I'm right."

Josh's look was thoughtful, rather than smug, and it almost made Connor wish he had opened up to him.

When Connor got back to Paradox Lake, he decided to check in with the church secretary to see how the pageant programs were coming before going home to work on his Christmas sermon. As soon as he pulled open the front door, he could hear the chatter of the day-care-center preschoolers in the church hall and Karen Hill's voice.

"Everyone find a place at the table. We're going to make a Christmas surprise for our mommies and daddies."

He thought about Hope's Christmas surprise for him. Ginger was settling in the house nicely, so nicely she hadn't shown a bit of interest in going back outside. They'd come to a sort of truce about climbing the Christmas tree. She only climbed it when he wasn't in the room to catch her. He'd made an appointment for the vet to check her out late this afternoon when Hope would be home from school, so she could come with him. Maybe he should ask the vet how well the cat would adapt to moving to Chicago. He'd heard cats didn't relocate well. He walked into the small office that adjoined his.

"Pastor Connor." Mary Hazard, the church secretary, scooped several pages off the printer and turned them print side down on the desk. "I didn't know you'd be in your office today."

Obviously. What could she be printing that she didn't want him to see?

"You usually don't have office hours on Wednesdays," she stammered.

"I was out and decided to stop in to see if you had the pageant program done. Is that it?" He pointed at the pages she'd taken from the printer.

"No, the program's right here." Mary picked up a

sheet from the other side of the desk and moved so she was blocking his view of the pages she'd taken from the printer.

He took the offered paper and reviewed it, uncomfortable with Mary's secretive behavior. "This looks great."

"Thanks," Mary said. "I've got all the other church work done. I can run the program over to the printer if you want. I'm going into Ticonderoga this afternoon anyway."

Her gaze darted to the doorway, as if she was waiting for someone. Had she been using church supplies to print something for someone else? That didn't sound like Mary. Maybe it was something for herself and she'd brought her own paper. But why hide it? She volunteered her time as secretary, so no one would begrudge her using the printer.

"I'd appreciate it." He handed the program back to her.

Mary looked from him to the door.

Waiting for him to leave? Still bothered by her actions, he opened his mouth to ask. The sound of the church's heavy wooden front door opening and closing, followed by footsteps in the hall, stopped him. He waited to see who it was.

"Pastor Connor." Tom Hall stopped short in the doorway. "I didn't expect to see you here today."

A man could get a complex here.

"But since you are, let's go in your office."

Mary handed Tom her "secret" sheets as the two men passed by her to enter Connor's office.

"Have a seat," Connor said, unease warring with his curiosity about what was going on. Tom *was* the chairman of the administrative council. Had Mary been nervous because she knew something he didn't want to hear?

Tom slipped into the chair and placed the pages on the desk. "I could have told you yesterday, but I wanted to have it all official first."

The word official made Connor think this had to be about his contract renewal. Tom's expression didn't give him a clue as to what he was going to say about it, though. Connor sat opposite Tom and tapped his toe under the desk as he waited for the man to speak.

"At the council meeting Monday night, we voted unanimously to offer you a three-year contract, effective January 31. It's all here." Tom pushed the contract across the desk.

Connor flattened his foot to the floor with a slap. "For real?" he asked, not caring that his question didn't sound very professional.

Tom nodded. "Some of the council members got wind that you have another offer elsewhere."

He hadn't shared that information with anyone other than Natalie. Claire... Claire was on the council. Nat must have told her. For once, he was thankful for the church grapevine.

"The possibility that you might leave us brought the couple of members who aren't your biggest fans into line." Tom dropped his voice. "Personally, I think those people like to oppose the pastor, whoever's called to the position."

"Thank you," Connor said, the elation rushing through him making him unable to say more.

"Take your time. Read it over," Tom said. "We realize how busy you are the next couple of weeks. We don't need your answer until after the first of the New Year.

I hope you do re-up with us, but I understand if your other offer is a better opportunity."

The two men shook hands, and Tom left. Connor pumped his fist. A three-year contract. What could be better? He fell back into his chair.

A life with Natalie, who was in Chicago auditioning for the job she wanted.

Yesterday and today had reminded Natalie of how much she liked being in front of the camera. The exhilaration, the satisfaction of doing something she thought could make a difference, and doing it well. She was aligned with the station's vision for the Good News segment, and the second part of her audition today had surpassed yesterday's segment, even to her most exacting critic—herself. According to the viewer voting stats, she'd aced the competition last night. She couldn't wait to see today's film clip broadcast and her numbers tonight.

Natalie unlocked her hotel room and dropped her Chinese takeout on the desk, glad to be finished at the station for the day. While her on-camera performances had been a dream, working with the station staff had been more of a challenge. She'd had to get past the looks and block out the whispered comments about her and her former mentor, Kirk, that some of the news staff had made no effort to hide. The tension had been palpable at the obligatory kick-off viewing party last night, which began at the start of the six-thirty newscast and lasted through the eleven o'clock one.

Tonight she'd begged off the informal viewing get-together with a headache, a headache that had relieved itself by the time she'd walked to the nearby restaurant for her takeout. After removing her coat and kicking off her boots, she situated herself cross-legged on the bed with her food and cell phone. She'd barely gotten to talk with Connor yesterday before the viewing party, and he'd been very quiet through the whole call.

Thinking about it now, it was probably because she'd enthused on and on about her day and hadn't let him get more than a word in at a time. Then she'd had to cut him off to go to the viewing. Tonight she had the whole evening free. Natalie opened her broccoli chicken and unlocked her phone to see a missed call from Connor a few minutes earlier. She'd had the phone on vibrate and must not have heard it buzz when she was walking back to the hotel.

Smiling in anticipation of hearing his voice, Natalie called him back.

"Hi," he said, picking up after the first ring.

"Hi. Sorry I had to cut our call short yesterday."

"I understand. Work is work."

She tightened her grip on the phone at his repetition of the words she'd used the other day when he'd had to shorten their time together because of his hospital visit.

"Did the segment go as well today as yesterday?"

"Better. And my viewer votes for yesterday's clip are phenomenal."

"Great. When do you have to be to the viewing tonight?"

Her bite of chicken stuck in her throat. Had she picked up a tone of resentment in his voice, or was she being hypersensitive? "I don't. I have the whole night free to talk about anything you want."

The phone went silent, and she checked to make sure they hadn't lost their connection.

"Unfortunately, I'm not free. I have to be at the church for the singles group Christmas party in a half hour."

Was Connor saying that because she'd had to go to the viewing party yesterday? Her party was work. She snapped the lid back on her chicken, the throb of her returning headache knocking out her appetite. His commitment was work, too, but he was essentially his own boss. No one was making him go.

"I need to talk with you about something, though."

"Sounds important." She tried to keep her tone light.

"The administrative council offered me a new three-year contract."

What little she'd eaten churned in her stomach. "Is it what you want?"

"I have until the beginning of January to decide."

In her mind, Connor's nonanswer was an answer. "The same as the offer for the assistant pastor position here." She couldn't stop herself from pointing it out.

"Yes. I'm still praying on it, but I'm feeling strongly that I'm supposed to stay at Hazardtown Community Church at least a while longer."

"Oh." Natalie knew he deserved more of a response, but she was at a loss what to say. She rubbed her temples.

"And, Nat." His voice was barely audible. "I want you with me."

The hotel room felt like it was closing in around her. "Are you asking me not to take the job here with the station if it's offered to me?" She bit her lip, half of her hoping he'd say yes, so she wouldn't have to make that decision herself, and the other half ready to accuse him of trying to get back at her by forcing her to choose between him and her career again.

"No. We have to take the path our Lord has for us.

He may have a reason you're supposed to be in Chicago and I'm supposed to be in Paradox Lake."

The throbbing in her head increased.

"Nat, you still there?"

"Yes."

"I've got to head out now. I love you," he said under his breath before hanging up.

Not knowing or caring whether he'd actually said the words, she whispered, "I love you, too" into the dead phone.

She closed her eyes and bowed her head. "Thank You, Lord." She finally had her answer.

Chapter Thirteen

Natalie rushed around the hotel room, throwing her belongings into her suitcase. The headache medicine she'd gotten from the convenience shop in the hotel lobby had helped her sleep so well, she'd slept right through her alarm this morning. She turned her cell phone on to call a taxi to get to the station for the meeting announcing the winner of the audition blitz. Her eye went right to the missed-call icon. Apparently, she slept through a return call from Connor last night, too.

"Natalie, call me back. I was kind of a pompous jerk last night, hanging up without letting you talk first. I'm not going to make the same mistake I made back in college. I know if we talk, we can work things out and come up with a solution. I love you."

Her heart soared. She was too frazzled to call Connor back this morning, and what she had to say was better said in person. She didn't want to leave her words open to any misinterpretation. She shot off a quick text—see you tonight—and called the taxi company.

Fifteen minutes later, she was in the station lobby, debating whether to take time to stash her luggage in her temporary dressing room and be even later for the meeting, or go right to the conference room, where the station manager was going to announce the winner of the audition blitz. She planned to go directly to the airport following the announcement and a brief appearance at the luncheon celebration afterward.

After a glance at the overhead clock, she opted for dragging her luggage along. It seemed every eye in the room was on her as she gingerly pushed open the conference room door. The station manager stopped his presentation while she slid into a seat in the back, making her wish she could hide under the chair.

"With Kirk gone, she's going to have to lose her 'I'm special' attitude if she thinks she's going to work here again," a news writer a couple of seats away said, not bothering to lower her voice.

Natalie clutched her hands in her lap.

"As I was saying—" the manager had resumed talking "—our initial data show both the audition blitz and the Good News segment were well received by our viewers." He clicked through voter and viewer demographics on the screen beside him. When he'd finished, he individually thanked the staff members who had worked on the project, along with the three women vying for the job. "Now," he said, "here's what you're all waiting for." The screen changed to pictures of Natalie and the two women she was competing against. With exaggerated drama, the station manager clicked and the competitors' votes appeared under their pictures. Third place. Second place. First place.

Natalie leaped to her feet. She'd won. By viewer popularity, she'd been voted in as the new Good News reporter.

"Congratulations, Natalie." The manager waved her up while the others in the room began clapping with varying degrees of enthusiasm. He directed her to the microphone at the podium.

She stepped behind it and smoothed out the paper with the speech she'd scribbled in the taxi on the way from the hotel. But she didn't need it. At the signal from the cameraperson in the back of the room, she began, "I can hardly express how thrilled I am with the viewers' decision, and I want to thank everyone here for helping me be at my best for the competition." Natalie paused. "Unfortunately, another commitment forces me to decline the Good News reporter position." She focused on the second place contender, whose eyes widened before she broke into a wide smile. "And," Natalie concluded, "thanks again to everyone for this opportunity."

The room went quiet before erupting in a din of conversations Natalie only heard as fragments. She nodded to the station manager, who stood openmouthed beside her, before she made her way along the side wall to her luggage by the door. She avoided eye contact with anyone else and made an on-the-spot decision to skip the luncheon entirely. Yes, she was running again. Only this time she was running *to* something.

Natalie stepped out of the station building and breathed in the cold winter air, a cleansing contrast to the stuffiness of the conference room. She flagged a passing taxi. "O'Hare, please," she said.

In the short time she'd been inside, snow had blanketed the sidewalk and streets. Getting to the airport early could be a good thing. Maybe she could get an earlier flight and fly out before the weather got worse, if it was going to get worse. She rifled in her bag and pulled out her cell phone to check the weather forecast and call Connor. Now that she'd done the deed, she felt she could talk to him on the phone and make her message clear. It was simple. She loved him and wanted them to be together, as he'd said last night. Natalie pushed the power button and got nothing but a blank screen. The battery was dead. Frustration at not being able to reach Connor gnawed at her the rest of the way to the airport.

The first thing she saw when she walked into the airport were the airline arrival-departure signs flashing weather-delayed and canceled flights. Relief flooded Natalie. Her flight was still listed as on time. Once through security, she dug through her suitcase for her phone charger. It wasn't there. She must have left it at the hotel. Locating a pay phone, she retrieved enough change from the bottom of her bag to call Connor's cell phone. She tapped her foot to the rings for what seemed like at least ten minutes, waiting for either him or his voice mail to pick up. Instead, she got a no-service recording. She hung up the phone and stared at it. Either he was out somewhere with no cell service, or this was one of the many times the service in the church-parsonage area had gone dead.

She racked her brain. What was the parsonage or church number? She hadn't a clue, so she called directory assistance and got both. But she was out of change. The phone hadn't returned her change from the uncompleted call to Connor's cell phone. Maybe she could use her debit card. After the third unsuccessful try, Natalie put her card away. Either debit cards didn't work, or the debit/credit-card feature was out of order.

Natalie trudged up the airline terminal to get change at one of the stores at the other end. "Great," she muttered when she looked at the arrival-departure sign she was passing. Now her flight was among the delayed ones.

"Natalie Delacroix, is that you?"

She swung around toward the voice. "Michelle," she said, recognizing the woman who'd produced the news at the last station Natalie had worked at. Shortly before the format change that had cost Natalie her job, Michelle had left the station when her husband had taken a position outside of New York City. "What are you doing in Chicago?" Natalie asked.

"Exactly what I was going to ask you," Michelle said. "Well, not what are you doing in Chicago, but what are you doing at the airport. Flying home to see your family?"

"No, an audition for a job. I've been home for a few weeks helping my mother while she recovers from knee surgery."

"How'd the audition go?" Michelle asked.

"I got the job, but I turned it down. I've decided to stay in Upstate New York, near my family."

"God works in interesting ways," Michelle said.

Natalie tilted her head in question.

"I produce a syndicated Christian Women's program in New York City, and our secondary cohost is leaving. Before you walked by, I was sitting here wondering how to get a hold of you. I think you're a good fit for the position. We record the segments for the whole month in a couple of days. I set things up that way so I get more time with my daughter. Generally, you'd only have to come down to New York from the Adirondacks for the recording days. Are you interested?"

"Definitely." It took all of Natalie's self-control not to punctuate her answer with a *wahoo*.

"Join me, and I'll give you more details."

Natalie squeezed the handle of her suitcase. Michelle was right. This had to be the Lord's work. "Can you give me a minute? I have to get some change to make a phone call. My flight's been delayed, and my cell phone died."

"Use my phone," Michelle said.

Natalie hesitated, uncomfortable with Michelle, a potential boss, listening to her talking to Connor.

Michelle handed her the phone and waved at an empty corner of the gate. "You can take it over there for privacy."

"Thanks, I'll be right back."

Natalie stood in the corner watching the blizzard outside while she waited for her calls—first to the parsonage and then to Connor's office—to go through. She got his voice mail both times. She left him the same message at each number. "Hey, it's me. My flight has been delayed because of blizzard conditions here. Hope you're having better weather there. I'm calling from a friend's phone. Mine died, and I must have left my charger at the hotel. I'll call back as soon as I know when I'll be getting into Burlington. Don't worry about the pageant. The flight's only delayed two hours." *For now, at least.* "And, I may have some good news on the job front." Natalie couldn't keep the excitement out of her voice. "Love you."

That excitement continued to bubble through Natalie as she walked back to where Michelle was sitting. Everything was falling into place. Connor could accept Hazardtown Community Church's three-year contract, and it looked like she might have a great job opportunity that wouldn't take her away from Paradox Lake—a job that would leave her time to be the pastor's wife, if Connor proposed again. If he didn't, she'd propose to him. All she had to do was keep her promise and be back for the Christmas pageant tomorrow night.

"And, I may have some good news on the job front. Love you." Connor replayed the message on the parsonage phone that Natalie had left hours ago. The first time he'd played it, he'd been jazzed by her "love you." Now, well past the time her plane would have arrived with a two-hour delay, he focused in on the excitement in her voice about the job. It had to mean she'd won the audition blitz and accepted the job in Chicago, without talking with him first. Shades of her first job. He'd told her about his offer from Hazardtown Community Church and that he'd probably accept it. But he hadn't planned on making a decision until she was home and they'd talked about it.

He tapped his finger on his renewal contract. The council had a couple of new benefits that skewed toward a pastor with a family. He and Natalie must have been more obvious at the open house than he'd thought. Had that weighed into the change of heart of the council members he'd been sure would oppose his contract renewal? What would they think of a pastor whose wife was only here weekends at best? He still had the offer from his friend, but his heart wasn't in it.

Connor began dialing the number to hear Natalie's voice mail again to see if he could read her voice any better. He punched the off button when he heard a car pull in the driveway. Maybe Natalie had run in to someone from Paradox Lake at the Burlington airport, gotten a ride home and was stopping in to surprise him. Connor tossed the phone on the couch in disgust. He was one lovesick puppy, coming up with that scenario to explain Natalie not having called him since early this afternoon. But he didn't want to let himself think that history was repeating itself, that she'd gotten the job and was having second thoughts about them.

The front door opened and Josh breezed in on a gust of wintry air. "It's a cold one out there tonight." He pulled off his ski cap and stuffed it in his coat pocket.

"What brings you out this way?" Josh wasn't the type to drop in without a purpose, especially on a Friday night.

"I was over at Sonrise, dropping off a prop for the pageant that I worked on at home. I saw your lights on, so I stopped. I thought you and Natalie would be out doing something tonight after you picked her up from the airport."

"How did you know I was supposed to pick her up?" Gossip-wise, sometimes being the pastor was almost as bad as being the town drunk's kid.

"Claire."

Was Claire why Josh wasn't at the Strand "helping" Tessa show this weekend's movie? Josh doing his usual hit-and-run on Natalie's sister made him uneasy, not that it was his business. "Nat's flight's been delayed because of a storm. I'm waiting to hear back from her." *And have been for hours.* "What were you dropping off at Sonrise? I thought you and Drew had everything there at dress rehearsal Tuesday."

Josh looked sheepish. "Hope said the cradle the Hazards lent the Sunday school for the manger scene didn't look like the 'real' one in the Bible storybook you gave her. So I told her I'd make her one like the picture in her book before tomorrow."

"Indulge her much?" Connor asked, glad for the diversion Josh was providing.

"Whenever I can." Josh peeled off his coat. "Gonna ask me in?"

"Be my guest." Connor motioned to the couch.

His brother made himself comfortable, picked up the remote and flicked on the TV, channel surfing until he found a basketball game. "I could use a cup of coffee."

"The K-Cups are in the cupboard above the coffee-maker."

Josh unfolded himself from the recliner. "You want one?"

"No. Thanks." Connor sank into the couch. He was on edge enough about not knowing what was going on with Natalie. He didn't need coffee or to deal with this strange pod creature who was impersonating Josh.

"What was that? A junior varsity freshman could have made that shot," Josh said to the television as he returned, placing his coffee mug on the table next to the recliner.

"Out with it," Connor said.

"What?" Josh asked between plays.

"Why are you really here?"

"Watching out for you, baby bro."

Connor could think of several times he could have used Josh's concern. This wasn't one of them.

"I was talking with Claire—"

"Your latest pursuit?" Connor interrupted. He felt bad for Tessa, who really seemed to like Josh. She put up with his company regularly. Connor knew how rejection felt. Justified or not, he was feeling it now. Of course, since

Josh was closemouthed about everything that wasn't a brag, Conner had no idea what his brother and Tessa's relationship was.

Josh leaned back in the chair and crossed his ankle over his knee. "Haven't decided. Of course, if her sister sticks around…"

Connor clenched his hands, even though he knew Josh had to be saying that to get a rise out of him.

Josh eyed his clenched fists. "Worse than I thought." His expression softened.

Connor unrolled his fists.

"You'll make a lot of your parishioners happy. Of course, as soon as you're married, half the congregation will start looking for the babies."

"I haven't said anything about marrying Natalie."

Josh waved him off. "It's written all over you."

Connor leaned back against the couch cushion. "Don't you want to settle down someday?" he asked to deflect the conversation from him.

"The only reason I can see for getting married is kids. Go forth and multiply and all that."

Connor worked a muscle in his jaw at the way Josh tossed out his version of scripture. He wanted to understand his brother. This was starting to be the closest thing to a real conversation he and Josh had had in years. But, as usual, Josh's attitude wasn't making that easy. "You don't want kids?"

The lines bracketing Josh's mouth deepened. "You know I don't. I have too many of Dad's bad characteristics. It's hard enough keeping them in control with adults. I'd be a terrible father."

He felt sorry for Josh, but he had a point. Josh was the most impatient of the three of them and the least tied to family. And he could see their father in the way Josh put himself first and was never happy with what he had, was always looking for the next best thing.

"I'm safe with Hope. I can be an indulgent big brother. I don't have to be responsible for seeing she grows up right." Josh avoided his gaze and emptied his coffee mug. "You're awfully quiet. Having second thoughts?"

Connor thought about last Saturday when he and Natalie had taken Hope and Robbie on the Polar Express and how he'd liked the way the four of them had felt like a family.

"No, you've got me. I want it all. Marriage, kids. No second thoughts." He glanced from the clock on the DVR to the phone. But he couldn't say the same for Natalie. Maybe he should have some doubts.

Natalie twisted her neck to work out the crick she'd gotten from falling asleep in the airport chair and adjusted her eyes to the too-bright lights. She looked at Michelle, who was still asleep in the seat beside her. She hadn't wanted to wake her last night to ask to use her phone. So instead, she'd used a pay phone to try to reach Connor and had lost the last of her cash in the pay phone attempting the call. Once she explained, Connor would understand her silence. *He had to.*

Michelle rustled beside her and shot up straight in the chair, wide-awake. "What time is it? I fell asleep. We haven't missed our flight, have we?"

Panic filled Natalie. Her gaze shot to the overhead arrival-departure sign. "No." Her unease escalated. "It's been canceled, and I've got to get home today."

"Me, too," Michelle said. "I can't miss my baby's first Christmas. Let's rent a car. I grew up in the snow belt south of Buffalo and you're from the mountains. We know how to drive in snow, and if we leave now, you can make your pageant tonight."

Natalie might not like driving in snow, but she did know how. "All right." She stood and reached for her suitcase. If it would get her back to Connor in time for the pageant, she could do some snow driving.

After she'd called Connor yesterday afternoon, Natalie had talked to Michelle about the pageant and needing to get home for it, although not all of the reasons why.

"But…" Natalie's excitement lost steam. "I can't… I don't… I don't have any money to help with the rental, and you'll be going miles out of your way."

"Pay me back later. Whatever. Besides, I need you to help with the driving. If we alternate driving, I can rest and be okay to drive the final stretch downstate to my house alone."

"Thanks." Natalie couldn't come close to expressing how much Michelle's generosity meant to her.

The weather report Natalie caught as she waited in the car-rental area for Michelle to arrange the rental renewed her excitement and hope. The storm was a slow-moving lake-effect storm that, because they were heading east, they'd soon drive out of.

Michelle waved her over. "We're all set. I've called my husband. Do you want to call someone now or later? My phone has only about enough power for a couple more calls—yours and an emergency one if we need it. I couldn't find a working outlet in this airport that someone wasn't already using."

"Now, thanks," Natalie said. Since Michelle was driving the first leg—hopefully, until they drove out of the worst of the storm—she could call from the car. But she wanted to get her message to Connor as soon as possible. She checked the time on the cell-phone clock—4:30 a.m.—and decided to call the parsonage phone. As much as she wanted to hear Connor's voice, she didn't want to wake him up, and he'd be less likely to hear the phone ringing in his office a couple rooms away or downstairs in the living room.

"Hi, it's me," she said to the voice mail. "My flight's canceled. Don't worry about coming to Burlington to pick me up. I ran in to a friend at the airport." A police siren shrieked so close behind them in the parking garage that Natalie covered her other ear to muffle the sound. "We've rented a car and are driving back to New York. I should be there for the pageant. Can't wait to see you."

Natalie handed the phone back to Michelle, who turned it off, and she settled in passenger seat of the rental car for the first leg of the drive. She was going to make it. All that stood between her and Connor was the fourteen-hour drive home.

Chapter Fourteen

Connor clenched his jaw in frustration. He had come downstairs Saturday morning to find another missed call from Natalie on the parsonage phone. She'd called at four thirty. It was almost as if she was deliberately calling when she knew he wouldn't pick up.

He swallowed the bile that rose in his throat. If he loved her, he should give her the benefit of the doubt. But her words hadn't given him much encouragement. The airline had canceled her flight, and she didn't need him to pick her up at the airport. He got that. It was out of her control. But she hadn't said anything about his pageant, being sorry for missing it. Apparently, she was going to stay with some friend she ran in to at the airport. All he caught of the rest of her message over the sirens and commotion in the background was her casual "see you." Meaning what? Another rejection? See you around, sucker? When he'd called back the number Natalie had called from, his call had gone directly to the voice mail of someone named Michelle. He hadn't left a message.

Connor picked up the small gray velvet box from the

table next to the phone and controlled his urge to crush it in his hand. Natalie was turning him into a sentimental sap. Earlier in the week, he'd taken the ring from the safe deposit box at the bank, where it had sat for the past five years. Yesterday, he'd bought jewelry cleaner and polished it. Today… He pushed away his thoughts of what he'd planned to do today. Cupping the box in his hands, he sank to his knees, elbows resting on the seat cushion of the couch.

Dear Lord, what does this all mean? I thought I had Your answer. Are Natalie's actions telling me I have it all wrong? We're not meant to be together? He felt the weight of the ring in his hands. *Or are You telling me not to accept the Community Church's offer too quickly, to reconsider the assistant pastor position?* He paused and listened to the dead silence in the house and in his head. *Tonight, we're gathering to celebrate Your Son's birth. Please lift the weight from my heart, so that I can give You and Your Son the glory You deserve and the people attending the pageant the renewal they're seeking. Ever in Your service. In Jesus's name, Amen.*

He pushed himself upright, placed the ring box back on the table and lifted the phone receiver. He had to find a substitute for Natalie for the pageant tonight. Connor looked through his contacts for Andie's number.

"Hi," a girl's voice said at the other end of the phone when his call rang through.

One of the twins.

"Can I talk to your mom? It's—"

She didn't let him finish. "Mom, some guy wants to talk to you."

Connor heard Andie reprimanding her daughter for her phone manners.

"Hello, this is Andrea."

"Andie. It's Connor. I need a huge favor. Can you fill in for Natalie at the pageant tonight? Her flight from Chicago's been canceled and she's not going to make it."

"Oh, no. She must be so disappointed. She really wanted to do this."

Andie's unexpected reply calmed some of the turmoil inside him.

"Of course I'll fill in," she said.

"Do you want me to ask Drew Stacey to open the auditorium so you can come early to practice?" He held his breath that Andie wouldn't take offense, thinking he meant she wasn't as good as Natalie.

"That would be great."

"Thanks. I'll be there early, too. We can run through the solo once."

"Sure, if you think we need to."

"See you tonight." He turned off the phone. He had someone to lead the choir. At least one thing was going in his favor.

That evening Connor looked out over the nearly filled auditorium, a pang of regret shooting through him as he ended his perusal with Andie, not Natalie, sitting at the piano. He hadn't heard anything more from her all day. He closed his eyes and breathed in—*Jesus*—then out—*loves me*—in a calming prayer exercise he'd learned in seminary.

Connor faced the audience. "Welcome. It's great to see such a crowd here for the fifth annual Paradox Lake Association of Churches' Christmas pageant. I'm Connor Donnelly, pastor of…" Natalie stood in the open center door to the auditorium, wearing the dress and boots she'd worn to the open house at the parsonage.

His mouth went dry, and his heart smashed against his chest. *She'd come.*

He cleared his throat. "I'm the pastor of Hazardtown Community Church and your host tonight." He motioned to Natalie. "Our late arrival is our music director, the talented Natalie Delacroix." Their eyes met and held for a moment before she hurried down the aisle. *The only woman I ever have loved, or ever will love.* At that moment, he decided that if Natalie could do whatever she'd done to get from Chicago this morning to Paradox Lake tonight for his pageant, he could take the assistant pastor position and move to Chicago for her.

Natalie said something to her sister that Connor couldn't hear before Andie walked up the steps to join the choir, and Natalie took her place at the piano.

He dragged his gaze away from her and addressed the audience again. "Let's bow our heads in prayer." He cleared his mind of the words he'd written and memorized for tonight and spoke what was in his heart now. "Dear Lord, thank You for gathering us here tonight, so we can thank You for all the gifts You have given us, not the least of which is Your Son. The Son You gave to us all to wash away our sins and make us as innocent as that newborn wrapped in swaddling clothes and laid in a manger that night so long ago. The Son whose story we celebrate tonight. Amen."

"Amen," the audience echoed.

He lifted his head. "Now, our combined church choir will start that story with 'It Came Upon a Midnight Clear.'" Connor let Natalie's prelude and the choir's voices flow over him as he took his place on the stage with the choir and watched the Sunday school's Mary and Joseph walk down the aisle to the manger centered on the floor in front of the singers.

A few minutes later, when the Sunday school angels heralded Christ's birth, Connor left his place with the choir to go stand by the piano for his and Natalie's "O Holy Night" solo. Before he reached the aisle between the risers, Andie startled him by stepping out of her choir spot and preceding him down the stairs. Natalie stood, giving Andie the piano bench. *So, that's what Natalie and Andie had been talking about before the pageant began.* Natalie joined Connor beside the instrument. The smile she gave him almost made him lean against the instrument for support.

He sang to her as if they were the only ones in the room and she sang to him, filling Connor with the joy of the season he'd had trouble finding earlier. When they finished the last chorus together, the audience went silent for a moment before breaking into a standing ovation. The loud reminder that they weren't alone halted his impulse to grab Natalie's hand and squeeze it. The rest of the program passed like a dream, punctuated by the usual mishaps that characterize any presentation involving small children but make those performances more endearing.

Afterward, Connor smiled until his face hurt, shaking hands and talking with the many people who came forward to congratulate him, all of the time impatiently wishing he could tell them they needed to go home so he could talk with Natalie. He pressed his palm against the jewelry box in his suit jacket pocket under his choir robe. Finally, the auditorium cleared, except for Natalie and him.

"I'm so glad you made it." He hugged her shoulder.

"You said your flight was canceled. How'd you do it?" His heart swelled with the unspoken knowledge she'd done it for him.

She tilted her head. "We drove, like I said in my message."

"So that was what you were saying when the sirens were blaring."

"You didn't know? You weren't expecting me?"

He shook his head, ashamed he hadn't had more faith in her. "I have to drop my choir robe and a couple other things off at church. I'll walk you to your car. Then meet me at the parsonage so we can talk."

"I can't do that."

Connor choked.

"I don't have a car. The friend I drove home with dropped me here before she headed to her house downstate."

"That. Was not. Funny. You could give a man a heart attack."

She smiled an innocent little grin that was just as lethal. "I'll get my coat and luggage."

Connor removed his choir robe and waited while she put her coat on. He carried Natalie's suitcase with one hand and opened the door for her with the other. After locking the door, he turned to walk her to his car. Their gazes locked.

"I got the Good News reporter job, but I turned it down," Natalie blurted.

"I've decided to take the Chicago job," Connor said at the same time.

They both burst into tension-relieving laughter.

"For me?" she asked.

"For you," he admitted. "Did you turn down the reporter job for me?" He held his breath. He shouldn't have asked, but old Connor had to know.

"Not entirely. I wasn't comfortable there, even though I loved the on-camera work. Some people couldn't let go of my past."

"But you have." Rather than being hurt that he wasn't the whole reason, or maybe even the main reason, she'd turned down the job, the thought that she'd finally forgiven herself filled him with intense joy and a feeling of rightness.

"I think so," she said, her awe showing in her voice. "But, wait." She touched his arm. "You haven't turned down the Community Church contract, have you?"

"No, why?" he teased.

"Because I love you. I realize I always have."

Hearing those words he hadn't heard from her in person for more than five years nearly knocked his feet out from under him. "I love you, too." His voice sounded rusty, as if he hadn't used it in a long time.

A smile tugged at the corners of her mouth. "And my home is in Paradox Lake now, not Chicago. I have a super job opportunity in New York City that would take me away from home only a few days a month," she said.

"You have another job offer that you could commute to from here?" He needed to make sure he'd heard her right.

"I do." Natalie told him about Michelle's talk program and offer.

"Then, you're going to stay here?"

When she nodded, Connor dropped to one knee on the snowy sidewalk.

"Aren't you cold?" she asked, eyeing him as if she'd just noticed he had on only his suit jacket.

"Not at all." He looked up at the face of the woman he loved with all his heart and at the North Star, the Christmas Star, shining overhead, a beacon in the jet-black sky. He drew the jewelry box from his pocket. "Natalie Delacroix, will you do me the honor of becoming my wife?"

"Yes."

Her simple response sent a shot of adrenaline through his veins. He'd never felt more alive. He lifted the ring from the box and slipped it on her finger.

Natalie stood statue-still for a moment, looking at her hand. "Yes," she repeated. "Now get up before you freeze to death and give me a welcome-home kiss."

He rose, ignoring the chill of the wind blowing against his wet trouser leg, and brushed his cold lips against hers, warming them both. As if he had any other choice.

Epilogue

"Merry Christmas."

The roomful of Delacroix family members greeted Connor when he stepped through the door as if they hadn't just wished him a happy holiday two hours ago at church. Natalie's father closed the door behind him, and Connor searched for Natalie among the smiling faces. He found her peering around the dining room doorway and his heart skipped. Slipping off his jacket, Connor pulled at the neck of his sweater. Had she told them? Or was this the family's usual holiday exuberance? He tried to remember back to the few holidays he'd spent with Natalie's family. His mind was blank. Proposing to Natalie last night had been easy compared to what this afternoon looked like. What did he know about happy family holiday celebrations?

As if sensing the source of his unease, Natalie pointed to her bare hand and shook her head slightly—*no*. They'd agreed to wait and tell her family together. Everyone's eyes seemed to be on him. Maybe it would have been better if she'd gone ahead and told them. Yeah, told them and let him know their reaction. Then he wouldn't have to suffer through dinner and the family's gift exchange waiting for The Moment, wondering what it would do to the warm holiday mood.

"Is that Connor?" Claire shouted from the kitchen.

"Yep," Natalie shouted back, her gaze trained on him, mouth curving in a slow smile that jacked up his already pounding heart rate to triple time.

He jerked his head to the side toward the front room, where the Christmas tree was. If he could get Natalie alone, maybe he could talk her in to going to Jared and Becca's for dinner as he'd originally planned. The invitation was still open.

"Then we're all here," Claire's said. "Dinner will be out in a minute."

Natalie wove her way through her brothers and sisters and their families, who were heading in the opposite direction into the dining room. She took his hand and threaded her fingers through his. Connor's gaze shot to the back of her father's head.

"Come on," she said with a grin. "It's not like this is the first time you've had dinner with my family."

"Yeah, but that was before."

"Having second thoughts?" There was a hint of a quiver to her tease.

He squeezed her hand. "Not on your life."

She led him into the dining room. Her grandmother, dad and most of the rest of the family were already seated at the table, leaving the two seats next to her father the only empty ones together. Natalie took the one farther away, putting him next to Mr. Delacroix. He tried to get comfortable in the wooden chair. What was with him? He liked Natalie's father. Her father liked him, or at least he seemed to. In the recesses of his mind, he remembered his mother saying his father had asked Grandpa for his blessing to marry her. Should he have done that? Should he do that? *No*, people didn't do that anymore. Did they?

"Hey, Connor, good to see you." Natalie's older brother, Marc, walked into the dining room from the kitchen carrying an enormous turkey and saving Connor from his thoughts.

"You, too. I see they put you to work."

"Occupational hazard." Marc took the seat next to his wife and toddler daughter.

"New restaurant going well?" Connor asked.

"Great."

Natalie's mother, along with Claire, Andie and her twins, filed in, carrying the rest of the food.

"Hope you don't mind if I say grace," Natalie's father said. "Family tradition."

"Not at all," Connor said. He would *not* read anything in to that.

Natalie's father blessed the food and gave thanks for all of the family's good fortune the past year, ending with "Thank You for bringing Natalie home for the holidays." With his "amen," the room broke into a din of conversation and clinking forks and clunking serving dishes.

When dinner ended with the promise of pie and coffee after the gift exchange, they moved in a mob to the front room. Natalie grabbed them a seat on the couch beside her mother, while he settled Grandma Delacroix in a side chair. The twins began bringing gifts over from the tree to make a pile next to Natalie's mom. She passed them out one by one.

As Connor watched, calm settled over him. Family. This was his and Natalie's future. He glanced at her. His heart squeezed. She appeared equally fixated on everyone opening their gifts, a dreamy smile curving her lips.

"Connor."

At his name, he leaned forward and looked past Natalie to her mother.

She smiled and handed him a rectangular-shaped present. "This one has your name on it."

He looked at Natalie, and she shook her head. The tag said it was from the Delacroixs. He hadn't even thought about getting Natalie's parents gifts.

"Go ahead and open it," her father said.

Connor tore off the paper. It was a bestselling thriller that he'd mentioned wanting to read at a church committee meeting her father had been at. He *knew* Nat's father liked him.

"Thanks. I can't wait to read it."

"All right, then. Everyone ready for pie and coffee?" Natalie's mother asked.

"Wait," Natalie said, as people started to rise. "There's one more gift. Connor's gift to me."

"I don't see anything left under the tree," Amelia said.

"No, I have it here," Natalie said.

Connor sucked in a breath.

Natalie held out her hand, displaying the sparkling ring on her finger.

"I'm so happy for you," Natalie's mother said, hugging her tight. She turned to Connor with tears of joy in her eyes. "Come over here." She opened her arms and gave him a hug, too.

"About time," her dad said, grinning at Connor.

He released his breath.

"Welcome to the family. I'm glad someone came up with a way to keep my girl here."

"Dad!" Natalie said.

"Well, I am."

Natalie's sisters and nieces swarmed him with hugs, and his future brothers-in-law slapped him on the back.

"Congratulations."

"Hope you know what you're in for."

His gaze traced Nat's profile, his heart swelling. He did.

After everyone had congratulated them, Natalie's mother shooed the rest of the family back into the dining room for pie.

Natalie leaned her head on Connor's shoulder and gazed softly at the Christmas tree. "I truly am home. For good." She lifted her gaze to him. "But Paradox Lake, Chicago, I'd be home anywhere you are."

Pure joy pulsed through him. A man couldn't want for anything more. He pulled her into his arms and kissed her with all the love he had, not caring who might walk in on them.

* * * * *

Dear Reader,

I love holiday stories, any holiday story, but particularly Christmas stories. They've been my favorite since I was young and my mother used to read my brothers and me *The Littlest Angel*. So I was thrilled when I received the go-ahead to set the second book in my The Donnelly Brothers series—Connor's story—during the Christmas season.

As it is for too many people, Christmas is a bittersweet time for Connor Donnelly and Natalie Delacroix. But, as Connor and Natalie find, it's also a time of renewal, a time when we're washed free of the past. In that spirit, I wish you and your family and other loved ones a happy and holy Christmas, filled with love and fond family remembrances.

Thank you so much for choosing *Holiday Homecoming*. If you enjoyed it, please sign up for my author newsletter at JeanCGordon.com. And feel free to email me at JeanCGordon@gmail.com or snail mail me at PO Box 113, Selkirk, NY 12158. You can also visit me at Facebook.com/JeanCGordon.author or Tweet me at @JeanCGordon.

Merry Christmas and Happy New Year,
Jean C. Gordon

REQUEST YOUR FREE BOOKS!

2 FREE INSPIRATIONAL NOVELS
PLUS 2
FREE
MYSTERY GIFTS

Love Inspired®